Being Possessed

Kotra Siva Rama Krishna

Published by Kotra Siva Rama Krishna, 2023.

BEING POSSESSED

First edition. January 1, 2023.

Copyright © 2023 Kotra Siva Rama Krishna.

ISBN: 979-8215820360

Written by Kotra Siva Rama Krishna.

Also by Kotra Siva Rama Krishna

Two Strangers On The Bed
A Girl's Conflict
Enna
Strawberry
Dusk
Just Relax!
Delicious Predicament
Nirupama
Half Opened Doors
Lovenest
Moonshine
Scarecrow
Closed Doors
Disturbed
Handfuls of Sand
Mansion of Illusions
Rain Flower
Rose Garden
Sand Dunes
Snow Flower
Split Personality
Being Possessed
Objection Sustained
House of Delusions
Rustle in the Leaves

Sasikala
Amaswitha
English Grammar Simplifier
Wisps of Smoke
Shadow in the Mirror
Love is Dangerous with a Stranger
Shadow of a Spirit
Unwanted Guests

License Notes

This book is licensed for your personal enjoyment only. This book may not be re-sold or given away to other people. If you would like to share this book with another person, please purchase an additional copy for each recipient. If you're reading this book and did not purchase it, or it was not purchased for your enjoyment only, then please return the same and purchase your own copy. Thank you for respecting the hard work of this author.

Disclaimer

The concept, plot, story, characters and everything in this novel are only fiction and emerged only out of the imagination of this author. If anything in this novel even a small part of it resembles, similar or identical to any living or dead or to any literature, anywhere in the world even remotely it is only coincidental and this author has no knowledge whatsoever of it and cannot take any responsibility for the same.

About me

I am an Indian English writer write mostly fiction books and so far I have written thirty books out of which twenty eight books are romantic, psychological thrillers and the remaining two are non-fiction books, Body, Mind and You and English Grammar Simplifier. The word count of my books range from 15,000 to 3,50,000 and the total word count of all my books is more than 30,00,000 (Thirty Lakhs Words). I have a weakness, I don't get the feeling that I wrote the book if someone else edits the same, so I am my own editor to all my books. As such there is a pretty chance that you may come across grammatical, verbal mistakes, incongruities and inconsistencies while going through my books, then please pardon me and go ahead. I am always open as much as possible when it comes to sexual narrations in my books as I think sex is very main and natural characteristic not just in human beings but in all other creatures also. So you can find sexual narrations in my books graphical, absolute and complete. My heart-felt thanks to all those who have been purchasing my books all along, encouraging me and supporting me.

Chapter-1

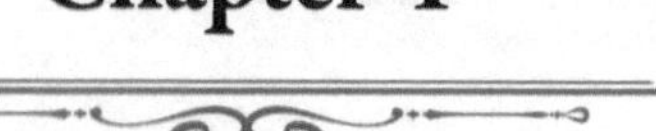

"At last we settled in our own home" Anand said looking around the flat in which they were then. "I just never hoped that we can own a house."

They entered into their flat one week or so before and it was arranged and furnished in all respects by then. As it was Sunday all of them were at home and after their breakfast settled themselves in the chairs and sofa there and talking in themselves.

"Don't forget there is a loan of forty lakhs rupees brother. Twenty thousand or so of amount we need to pay every month for nearly twenty years or so." It was Prathap brother of Anand said.

"Why the bloody hell you talk like that while we have been enjoying in our own home happily." Thanuja sister of Anand and Prathap was angry. "Our brother can easily clear that loan and you just forget about those financial responsibilities."

"I just want to ...." Prathap tried to say something more.

"Thanuja is right!" Anand's wife Malathi intervened. "You need not worry about our financial obligations and just concentrate on your studies. We do have comfortable amount in our hands even after meeting with all our financial necessities every month from your brother's salary. If there is necessity, I also do a job. I am a post graduate in English literature and don't forget about it."

"There is no such necessity and I just want you to be with my parents and looking after their welfare." Anand said looking into Malath's eyes.

"How do you people forget about my pension and the fixed deposits of your mother and I in the banks? If there is necessity I sure do give them and your mother also never does object to that." Anand's father Sudarshan said while looking into the face of his wife Sulochana.

"Do you need to say about it particularly? Everyone knows about it." Sulochana said mocking anger. "I really like Malathi staying in the home and looking after us and our children but........." she paused for a moment before saying again. "..............if she is interested to do a job, neither your father nor I would object to it."

"I am more interested in serving my family rather than doing a job." There was firmness in Malathi's voice. "Before marriage, Anand took a promise from me that I do look after the family and his parents staying at home and I have a habit of keeping my promises. Moreover ...." a small smile made her lips widened "............I really like doing that."

On hearing that all of them there laughed and Anand said after controlling his laughter. "In fact my company needed me more than I need that company. It compelled me to take the loan and buy this house only with the idea that I do bind with it until that EMI is cleared. It is a loan that I took from the company rather than from a bank."

"You are such a good person that they want to keep you like that." Sulochana said.

"That company is also a very good company aunty. It has good standing for more than forty years, earning good profits every year and its share price also is very strong and nice." Malathi said.

"You have such interest in share market that you track companies and their performance also." Anand said after looking into the face of his wife with an appreciative expression. "Malathi is right."

"Both your wife and mother' statements are right. That company and you both are good and want to cling to each other." Sudarshan said.

Once again everyone there laughed with happy expressions and once that laughter ceased to smiles Malathi said. "Though none of us do believe in spirits, I am feeling little uneasily considering the past history of this flat. The family of the tenant of this flat died like that! There are rumours that this flat is haunted and the one or two family who came into this flat on rent could not stay in it peacefully and eventually vacated it. Of course, I don't believe in spirits and paranormal but hearing it like that is creating little fear in me."

Anand laughed. "When paranormal itself is absolutely false and non-existent, how that rumour their spirits are still in this flat can be true?"

"My close fried Malavika believed in spirits and paranormal a lot. She became a para psychologist." Malathi said

"It is not important whether anyone else believes in paranormal or not. Tell me whether you have belief in it or not?" Anand knitted his brows together still keeping his gaze on the face of Malathi. "You also have agreed for purchasing this flat. Why you are talking like this now?

"Of course, I agree with it. You purchased this flat after taking my consent also and I don't believe in spirits and paranormal. But............." she paused for a second. "..........how our beliefs do anything with it if there are really spirits? If there are spirits in the world, they don't become non-existent just because we believe that they are non-existent."

"Tell me straight what you really want to tell." Anand's face was filled with irritation. "I cannot understand this type of indirect talking."

Malathi sighed heavily and said. "I don't want to talk in this way in a happy situation like this but I cannot remain without expressing my real feeling. I don't know why but I am feeling little uneasily in this flat from the moment I entered into it."

"Yes, not immediately but after one day or so of our entering into this flat I am also feeling uneasily." Anand's sister Thanuja said.

After that Anand's father Sudarshan, mother Sulochana and his brother Prathap also expressed similar feelings.

"I must be frank, I am also feeling little uneasily after entering into this house. But we have to notice one thing here! We heard about the accident of the car in which the family of the tenant of this house Swaroop and their instant death in it. We know about the rumours also even before purchase that their spirits are still in this flat. However much we don't believe in spirits and paranormal, our subconscious believes in them and creates such uneasy feeling in us. If your psychologist sister Saritha is with us now, she would have said the same thing." Anand said.

On hearing Saritha's name, a worrying expression instantly filled the face of Malathi. Saritha was the sister of Malathi three years younger to her. When Saritha was just five years old their mother died and their father married again. Their step mother who entered into their lives tortured them to the maximum and their father has to put maximum effort to get them educated and has to fight tooth and nail with their step mother to fix the marriage of Malathi with a nice guy like Anand who was not only educated but handsome also. But by the time of Saritha's marriage their father also died and their step-mother and half brother who took birth on the next year of their father's second marriage and their whole idea all the time was how fast they could get rid of Saritha. So in random they fixed her marriage with a guy who was easily available and as Saritha also was so much desperate to escape the torture from her step-mother and half-brother, agreed to that marriage. The husband of Saritha was a heavy drunkard and his lungs were damaged to the maximum by the time of marriage itself so just in six months of the marriage he died. In fact it was a big relief to Saritha her husband's death like that but the torture in the hands of her in-laws has become even more and she could not manage to stay there at all but her step-mother and half-mother firmly told her that they would never allow her into their house. The morning of that day also Saritha phoned to Malathi and told her how much she was being tortured by her in laws. Remembering all that the worrying expression in the face of Malathi has intensified even more.

"Why don't you ask that poor girl to come and stay with us? I already told you to tell her to come here and stay with us. Now we do own a house also." Sulochana said when Malathi said about the phone call of Saritha on that morning also. All the family members very well knew about Saritha and her hardships.

"Next time I talk to her, I certainly tell so to her aunty. I am also thinking that is the only way to save her from that torture." Malathi said and before anyone else would say anything as if to change the subject she said again "Every family in this apartment is good and invited me into their homes when I went but none of them are coming into our home. Even on house warming day also, only few people did come and they too did not stay long here. I can understand why they are doing so. They have been too much influenced by the ghastly death of that tenant's family and the later on rumours."

"You are right." Sulochana said. "I also have the experience just Malathi has. I am having a warm welcome into every home but I am not having any chance to welcome anyone like that into our home."

"I don't think each and every one in this apartment believing these rumours. It is our fault that we did not plan our housewarming in a grand manner. Just because of my busy schedule in the office, I planned it in a very simple way so the invitations also were just in a formal manner. Otherwise it would not have been like that." Anand said.

"I am not thinking like that........." Sulochana tried to say something more.

"Mom, what you really want to say?" Anand's face was once again filled with an irritating expression. "There is really something paranormal in this house to which those people are feeling fear and don't want to come?"

"No, of course. I just don't know.........." Sulochana was hurt on hearing her son so but really did not know what to say to that.

"Aunty just said about the reaction of the residents here which I also have felt in the same way." Malathi said little angrily. "Don't we have freedom even to express our feelings? For such simple thing you need not be irritated like this."

"I am sorry." Instantly there was a regretful expression in the face of Anand. "I just felt little irritated when you both expressed like this while we are so happy that we own a home for the first time in our lives. And.........." he paused for a second before saying again. "........we know about the death of that tenant's family and the rumours later on also even before purchasing this house. It was not completely unexpected the residents action in this way. Once we don't have any belief in spirits and paranormal, why do we feel fear?"

"Alright, alright. Forget about that matter for the present and we think about the matters that make us feel even more happy. This house is just in a walkable distance to Prathap's college and there is a park nearby to me to go and enjoy. The only thing which makes us worried is; it is little bit far to your office."

"I can manage the distance so easily in my car and it is not at all something that I need to worry about." Anand smiled and said. "After considering everything deep, I purchased this house. Otherwise, I would not have."

"I am also happy. The new college also is so good to me and I already made good friends there. I must say I am as much enjoying in the college as I am in the home." Prathap said.

Prathap has to change into a new college to study his second year master of commerce from his old college as the old college was too far from their new house. But as he said, this new college was so good and quite enjoyable to him.

"One other thing we have to feel so happy to remember here." Anand said. "Our flat is a three bedroom flat in the second floor and even a single bedroom flat in this apartment itself is more than one crore rupees. I inquired with the residents of this apartment and a three bedroom flat in this apartment certainly costs more than three crore rupees. Just because of the rumours and people believed in them, the owner of this flat sold it to me just for sixty lakhs rupees. It is just our good luck that owner is an uncle to my best friend and I came to know about he wanted to sell this flat at such a lower price! Otherwise, I don't think I would be the only person to jump to purchase this house at such a lower price."

"I have to agree with you." Malathi laughed and said and all the others there also laughed and once again there were happy expressions in their faces.

"In one or two months everything will be settled. Once people see our living happily in this house, they do start visiting our house." Anand said. "So we don't worry about anything else and just enjoy your lives here."

"Best suggestion in my opinion." Sudarshan nodded his head and said.

All of them there said 'yes' in union but everyone of them then was doing only one thing. That to cover the unknown uneasiness in them while trying to enjoy their stay there.

IT WAS ONE MONTH AND time was going by. Anand was going to his office, Prathap to his college, Malathi, Thanuja, Sulochana and Sudarshan spending their routines in their usual way. Thanuja completed her graduation one year back and as her family were too much fixed to perform her marriage as fast as possible she did not prefer to study anymore. So mostly she stayed home, helping her mother and *vadina* (brother's wife) in household chores while learning the same.

The one troubling thing which none of the family members could express to others was; the unknown uneasiness which started in them from the moment they entered into that flat. It was not because that the others would feel bad if they expressed it out but just because they could not analyse it at all and understand why they were feeling so. They just could not be convinced just because of their knowing about the death of that tenant's family like that and rumours later on, they were feeling so. The strange uneasiness was constant and in the same measure in them all the time.

"Saritha phoned to me." While Sulochana was busy at the stove and she was cutting the vegetables on the dining table with a knife, Malathi said to her. "No change in her life. She has been suffering a lot. Her parents in law are just torturing her all the time saying that their son was dead just because of her."

"How they can say it like that? Everyone knows how he died. He is a drunkard and because of his heavy drinking his lungs were damaged beyond repair and he died. What your sister can do for that?" Sulochana left the ladle in the pan, turned back and looked at Malathi.

"But her in laws are not thinking like that. They are thinking because of her he increased his drinking and ultimately died so."

"There is no more absurd thing than that! Anyhow it is your mother's mistake that she gave such a beautiful and intelligent girl to such a rogue! You people would have done more research on that family before making an alliance like that."

"You are absolutely right! But we cannot expect anything more than that from my step-mother." by then Malathi finished cutting the potatoes and pour the pieces of them into a small pot there with her hands. "All the time she just wanted to get rid of Saritha and agreed with him as he did not ask for any dowry and agreed to marry her in a simple way. The torture to Saritha in the hands of my step-mother has become unbearable so she just wanted to escape from that and agreed her marriage with that rogue. All the time I have become so helpless! If my dad was alive by that time, the situation would have been different."

Sulochana took the pot in which Malathi poured the potato pieces and said. "Anyhow there is no use in worrying about the past. She is still quite young, just twenty two years or so aged. She can remarry and lead a happy married life. We should concentrate on finding a good person for her atleast this time."

"I am also of the same opinion aunty." Malathi sighed heavily and said. "But she has to come away from that hell-hole first."

"I already told you to ask her to come straight here and stay with us. Once she is with us, we do try to find a suitable guy for her." With the same modulation Sulochana said. "There are men who can understand the widows and come forward to lead their lives with them. What all you need to do is; just put your effort in the right way. Upload her photo and details in all those marriage websites and apps. Do I need to tell this to a modern woman like you?"

"You are right aunty. I certainly do that." With firmness in her voice Malathi said. "My step-mother and her parents in law may never agree to it but I do try to settle her in her life again and I am confident about that."

"Once they don't like your sister at all, why do we bother about them? They may not give the share of their son in their properties to her but her settling in her life is more important than that. Don't worry about anyone and just concentrate on settling her in her life. First ask her to come to our home straight."

"I already told her to do that but she is reluctant. She is thinking it may be troublesome to me if she stays like that. But I force her to come here and stay with us. I think half of her problem would be solved if she comes and stay here with us." Malathi said.

"ON THE EVENING OF THIS day there is flat residents' meeting. I want to attend it." while they have been taking breakfast in the morning, Anand said. "So on this day there are no outings."

"As we are going out every Sunday, there is no problem in skipping one Sunday." Malathi said "Anyhow why did you fix like this to attend this meeting yourself? Anyone of us can attend it and know the proceedings."

"Even we have been residing in this flat so happily for more than one month, none of the residents in this apartment are preferring to come into our house. I just want to convince them that there is no wrong with this flat and they can so happily visit us."

There was sudden silence and all of them looked into each other's faces for few seconds. The odd uneasiness was just so in them all the time but none of them were interested in talking about it.

"Yes, that is indeed a nice idea!" after few seconds, breaking that silence Sudarshan said. "I also do attend the meeting if you have no objection to that."

"Even every family member of us does attend the meeting, I have no objection to it." Anand laughed and said.

"At what time that meeting is going to be held?" Malathi suddenly asked.

"Evening at six." Anand looked into the face of Malathi with a smile. "If you both mother in law and daughter in law don't want to become too much busy in the kitchen at that time, you can attend that meeting."

"Neither of us has such an idea but you have to do some help in before that. I know very well that you have no programs before six on this day." Malathi said.

"Don't kill me with suspense and tell me what that help I have to do?" Anand could not remain without expressing his irritation in his face. He wanted mostly to take rest in the home while watching T.V. on Sundays and if he has been asked to do any work on that day, it would irritate him a lot.

"You need to go to railway station to pick up my sister. She drops there by twelve o clock train and I am thinking it is better that you do take her from there along with her luggage in your car."

"You did not tell me that your sister is coming on this day." The irritating expression in the face of Anand was disappeared. Saritha not only more beautiful than his wife but active and intelligent also and he really liked Saritha a lot.

"She told now, is it is not enough?" Sulochana asked. "Just go by that time and bring her home in the most comfortable way possible."

Then Anand understood there was full agreement of her mother for his wife's sister's coming to his home. If it was so there was nothing in it to worry about.

"YOU JUST DON'T KNOW, how much I have been suffered all these days. If you have not invited me like this into your home, I am just planning to commit suicide." As soon as she entered into that flat and adjusted herself, Saritha burst into weeping hugging her sister Malathi.

"How you do think like that forgetting how I am going to be affected by that?" Malathi with force relieved herself from her hug and asked with a horrifying expression while looking into Saritha's face.

"What should I do? Mom and brother are not at all agreeing to my staying in their home. I just cannot bear the torture in the hands of my parents in law and sister in law. If you were in my place you would have understood my condition."

"I need not in your place to understand your condition. I know very well how much you have been suffering and we both don't expect even in our imagination also that our step-mom and half-brother let you enter into their house again." Malathi paused for a second and sighed heavily. "Thank God! You did not do any foolish thing! The best thing you are with us now and there is no necessity to you to worry about. Anyhow I am forcing you to come here for such a long time. You did not prefer to come until I forced you like that now. If the situation has become that much horrible, why did not you come in before itself?"

"Until the last time you told me I don't know that aunty also wants my staying along with you people. I know about aunty very well but without knowing her express consent like that I could not think to come here." With an uneasy expression in her face Saritha said.

"It was my mistake I did not tell about it in before itself." Malathi sighed heavily.

"Its alright. We better forget about the past and think about future." Sulochana said "We are having some plan about you if you are ready to severe all your connections with your in-laws. It may be too early to talk about our idea but I am thinking it is better that you do know about it as early as possible."

"I am just feeling disgust to think about anything of my in-laws and I am not feeling any relationship with them." Looking into the face of Sulochana, Saritha said. "My sister never could have allowed me into this house if you have not agreed to that. I know that you do think about my welfare. I am ready to agree to any plan you have for me."

"It may take some time to be implemented and there is no problem whatsoever to that and there will be no coercion also on you." Sulochana said. "We want to remarry you with a suitable guy. I am sure that there will be persons who can understand you and come forward to live happily with you."

"I did not think like that till this moment." Saritha said. "But a good woman like you who are thinking only for my welfare suggests it, I don't deny it."

"Alright. Everything is set." Anand said. "You go and take rest. I also go, take rest and be prepared for the evening meeting."

Chapter-2

"Everything is alright at present in our apartment and all the residents here are happy." Once they were all settled in the chairs on the terrace, the secretary of the association Mangal Rao said. "If any of you are having any problems, they will be sorted out."

To that meeting only Anand was attended as the rest of his family including Saritha were interested in going to a nearby temple. His father Sudarshan also changed his mind from his decision to attend the meeting and went along with them to the temple.

"In the night time, whenever the current has gone, the generator will not be put into operation immediately." One of the tenants, Niranjan said. "You know that power cuts have become quite often now a day here."

"Yes, yes. He is right." One other tenant, Chalapathi said. "It is sometimes taking more than twenty minutes to come power into our homes through generator."

"The generator has become old and it needs to be replaced. We are thinking that it is better to have a high capacity generator this time but we need to collect funds from you people for that matter. In fact this is one matter I want to discuss with you people now."

There was some silence among the people and they looked into each other's faces. "I have no objection to contribute. Make the calculation and tell me how much each flat owner has to pay." Chalapathi said

"I do that. The only problem is owners who are not the residents here may not be that much interested for contribution to buy a new and high capacity generator." Mangal Rao said.

"In the whole of our apartment there are only three tenant families and the rest of us are all owners. If those owners of the tenant's flats are not interested in contributing to it; we all the other owners have to contribute to the same. This generator problem has to be solved on priority basis." One other flat owner, Sundar, said.

"That much is true." Anand said as his family also was facing that problem. "I also contribute a little more than my share if there is necessity."

When Anand said that all the others there looked into his face and he just could not understand what expressions were they. He just could not understand whether they were pity, fear or something else.

"Alright then. We get a quotation for the high capacity generator and tell how much each of the owners has to pay. I shall see that this would be done as fast as possible."

After his saying like that there was few seconds silence until it was broken by Mangal Rao himself.

"It is two years that our new watchman joined in the duty with his family. So far I don't have any complaints from anyone as in the case of old watchman. All of you are feeling in the same way about this watchman or any of you feeling any difficulty?"

"Nice wife and husband both of them." Rajarao a tenant in the apartment said. "They attend any of the problems within minutes. We never can get such type of people if we let them go."

"Yes, yes, he is right." Almost all of them there have expressed the same opinion.

Anand also saw that watchman and his wife many a time. That watchman Manikyam was thirty years or so aged guy and his wife Chamanthi was twenty five years or so aged. They both had a three months or so aged daughter Nalini. Anand also just has the opinion as all the others there have and he expressed it just like that then.

"Are there any other problems you people are facing now?" looking into the faces of the people there, Mangal Rao asked them.

"Water is not coming out properly in our bathroom and I think some plumbing has to be done. Do you know any good plumber to settle that problem?" Annapurna who was one of the flat owners asked.

"I know and I send a good plumber to your home tomorrow itself, don't worry." Mangal Rao said.

"If you people are facing any other problems, just let me know." Mangal Rao said. "I don't want any of you people feel uncomfortable here."

"It is not about any problem but I want to make a proposal." Sravanthi one other flat owner who was there said. "We must have something like picnic somewhere. All the residents of this apartment should meet at one place and enjoy ourselves. It develops good rapport among all of us which will be quite beneficial."

"It is indeed a good suggestion! We sure do think about this." with a smile on his lips Mangal Rao said. "If there are no problems to discuss about and find solutions, we may conclude this meeting."

"I want to say something here." Anand got off from his chair and said that as he was waiting eagerly to say it "It is not about any problem and I am not making any proposal also. But I just do want to say something here."

"None of us do have any objection to hear whatever you say" Mangal Rao said with a smile on his lips. "Just express yourself."

"I know that no one among you is interested in coming into my flat. I am not blaming you anyone as I know the reason for it. You all people are thinking that the spirits of the deceased Swaroop's family members are still in my flat. You are feeling fear to those spirits and not coming into my flat. Even the watchman and his wife also are not interested in coming into my flat." Anand paused for a second before saying. "But you just see for more than one month, we family have been so happily residing in my flat. So none of you people need to feel any fear and come into my flat."

"On the housewarming day most of us have come into your flat, I just don't know why you are thinking like that!" with a surprising expression in his face Mangal Rao said. "We participated in the party hosted by you and took our lunch."

"Yes, but that party and lunch happened on this terrace not in my flat." Anand said. "And only few of you ventured to come into my flat not many. After that incident none of you are interested in coming into my flat despite my family members inviting you. All my family members are so much worrying about it." there was anxiousness in the face of Anand then.

"I ....I don't know what to say." There was sudden anxiousness in the face of Mangal Rao. "But I cannot rule out that the residents of this apartment are having particular fear to your flat."

"That is what I do want to expel. There are no spirits in my flat now and we are all so happy in that. Any of you may happily come into my flat. Please tell that watchman and his wife also that they can come into my flat and work for us."

"The problem relates to your flat is not as simple as you are thinking. We just don't know how you people can manage happily in that flat now but the tenants whoever came into it after that Swaroop's family vacating and died so could not stay in that more than one week." Mangal Rao said.

"If the problem with my flat is not as simple as I think, I just want to know how much complicated it is." With fresh anxiousness in his face Anand said.

"Mr.Anand........." Anand suddenly heard that voice, turned back and found Chakravarthy the opposite flat owner of his flat. "............you don't worry this gentleman. I hope I can supply all the information in that regard if you come into my flat."

"Why not, with pleasure!" Anand said. "I come into your flat now itself if you have no objection."

"Then come with me." Chakravarthi started walking away from that place and Anand just followed him.

"WE BOTH ARE GOING TO have some private talk in my room. Don't disturb us." Chakravarthy said to his family members, his wife Renuka, son Prasad and daughter Pallavi once he entered into his flat along with Anand.

After the three greeted Anand with smiles, Renuka said. "None of us are going to disturb you and you both can talk as long as you want."

"Nearly two years back that Swaroop's family came into rent into the flat in which your family is residing now. Swaroop, his parents, his wife and his brother and sister. They lived in that flat nearly one year and on one day they suddenly vacated it. After all the luggage etcetera has been sent out under some transport service, the whole of the Swaroop's family started from here in their car. After going some sixty miles or so from here, that Swaroop's car has been met with a huge accident and everyone of his family met with an instant death."

After settling themselves comfortably in the chairs facing each other in Chakravarthy's room, Chakravarthy started talking. Even he heard about that Swaroop and his family death like that in that accident before, hearing like that from Chakravarthy again increased the unknown uneasiness in Anand even more. He knew that there was more to come from Chakravarthy, so he remained silent.

"That man, Swaroop, used to work as a stock broker and he has his own office also for that. He made most of the residents of this apartment also to invest into the stocks he selected and I also invested. But after that a big slump has come in the stock market and most of the stocks we have invested went drastically down. The problem has come mainly because most of the people whom he made invest in the stock market did not know much about the stock market and they started pressurising him for the loss occasioned to them and he became very much stressed and strained. Not just with that problem, he started having other problems also and at one moment it has become quite impossible to him to bear them. So, as I said before, he left this place with his family like that and whole of his family died like that. The residents here, who invested in the shares he suggested and were in big loss also tried to stop him but he did not. If they could manage to stop him from going like that on that day, his family would have been alive on this day." Chakravarthy sighed heavily and leaned back in the chair.

"What is that much surprising in any of this?" Anand could not remain without asking in the small pause "What is that much paranormal in the whole of this to make you people to feel fear to come into my flat? However much unfortunate it is, so many people are dying every day and his family also died like that on that day."

"There is still something I did not tell you yet. After few days of their death like that we started hearing sounds from your flat. The voices of their people, their weeping and yelling! That Swaroop's family was not a peaceful family. There were always quarrels between the family members with loud voices quite disturbing to us neighbours especially in the night times. I just cannot say why those people did have those quarrels only in the night time. We just don't know how to understand while we were hearing their quarrels, weeping and yelling regularly in the usual times even after their death also. Mangala Rao secretary used to have the key of that flat with him and on one day that Mangal Rao, Muchikund the left side neighbour of you and I opened your flat and entered into it. Once we entered into it, we could not find anything in that but all three of us got very odd and uneasy feeling in us. We just could not stay more than five minutes in that flat, came out of that flat and locked it. On that day itself we three became seriously ill and could not be alright for one complete week. We three used to have dreams in which that Swaroop and his family members warned us not to enter into that flat ever again. That was why Mangal Rao said the problem related to your flat is not as simple as you are thinking."

On hearing that Anand remembered the uneasiness all his family members were feeling from the moment they entered into that flat. But why that Swaroop's family did not do any harm to them, why did not they make his family also seriously ill and warn them to go out of it?

"The previous flat owner who sold this flat to you, gave it on rent to two or so families after Swaroop's family vacating like that and none of them could stay in that flat for more than one week. Afterwards, hearing about the bad reputation of your flat, no people have come forward to take it on rent. If we are not the owners of our flat, we would have vacated this and went away a long time back. We would have sold our flat and go away but we bought it with lot of interest and by paying three crores and except that problem there is no problem to us. There are only three flats in this whole floor, big three bedroom flats each costs more than three crores at present, one occupied by you, two by my family and the other by Muchikund and his wife. There is no problem to other residents in this apartment but that Muchikund and my family used to face lot of problems because of the disturbance from that Swaroop's family while they were in that flat alive and after their death also. Even it was quite disturbing we did not feel fear to their disturbance while they were alive but we just don't know how to take it after their death. We used to feel lot of fear in those days and now also we are feeling some fear to your flat. Thank god, those disturbances have stopped completely after you people entered into that flat and we both families are quite thankful to your family for that."

Anand was about to say something but then Renuka, Chakravarthy's wife entered into the room with two tea cups and snacks in a tray.

"I am sorry that I have to disturb you both like this." While Anand was taking a tea cup with saucer and snacks from the tray she said and then put that tray before Chakravarthy and he also did just like Anand.

"In fact I want to thank your family. After your coming into that flat, we have been residing in our flat quite happily."

"Why it is so?" Anand's face was with a surprising expression but he could guess the reason.

"Just because there is no disturbance to us now from your flat. It is just like everything is normal in that flat at present."

"What does that mean everything normal?" Anand once again felt intensive fear in his heart. "What was that much paranormal before in that flat?"

"I am telling everything that is necessary and you need not tell anything. Just go into the kitchen and do your work." Looking into Renuka's face with an irritating expression Chakravarthy said.

Renuka nodded her head as if she understood the mistake she did and went away from that place.

"I just cannot say how you people have been living that happily in that flat now Mr.Anand but the tenants who resided in that after Swaroop's family could not stay peacefully even for one week." Once again looking into the face of Anand after his wife moving away from that place, Chakravarthy said.

"What are his family members?" Anand asked him.

"I already told you" Chakravarthy said "His aged parents, his wife, one brother and one sister."

"Just like my family." Anyhow Anand did not like what he heard. "I am also living with my aged parents, my wife, my brother and sister."

"Yes, I saw all your family members and talked with them also." Chakravarthy said "There is one other surprising thing in all this Mr.Anand. The ages of the both of you family members also are quite matching. That Swaroop was as much aged as you are, and his parents are also just like as much aged as your parents and for the rest of the family members also it is just like that."

The uneasiness in Anand has grown even more. "Can you say the main reason for the quarrels in his family?" he asked.

"There are more than one reason for the quarrels and all were equally main. One reason for those quarrels was their financial crisis. I already explained to you what happened to his share market business."

"I know about share market and I know how drastically it goes down on some occasions. I know the period when most of the companies' shares reached their bottom and I am thinking certainly it was then. My companies' shares also went down to all time lows and recovered later." Anand paused for a second as if to reiterate whatever he was going to say. "But he need not take responsibility personally for that and ran away from here so. None of the investors could sue him for the loss they suffered because of their share prices going down and he would have explained about that danger also to that investor as he is a professional stock broker."

"You are absolutely right Anand but you don't know about the larger public mindset. They do concentrate more on the rewards than the risks. He sure would have told about the risks to them as he did to me before making them invested but they did not concentrate much on that and invested their money only thinking about the profits. But once they suffered loss like that they started pressurising him so. And there is one interesting thing also here."

"Tell me what it is?" Anand has momentarily forgotten the growing fear in him and asked him curiously.

"Just in six months or so after his family members' death including him, the shares he made us invested came into profits again and all his investors were happy. Even some of the investors wanted to thank him but he was late along with his family by then." Chakravarthy gave a small pause. "But in those days the shares were quite low, the pressure was a lot on him and he was showing it on his family members. His wife also was quite sore with him as he was doing that business and made them all suffer. Some of his clients came to his house also and quarrelled with him and his family members. His share market business was one of the reasons for the quarrels in his family."

"It appears so." Anand nodded his head "Any other reasons for the struggles?"

"I know there were reasons but I don't know specifically what were those reasons. On the whole that Swaroop was not a good guy and it appeared none of his family members like him much. None of his family members liked him and quarrelled with him."

"I see" Anand said and leaned back in his chair.

"The other thing here is.........." Chakravarthy paused for a second and said "...........his parents also did have serious differences and disputes between them both. We used to hear that they both also quarrelled in between themselves on many occasions. Surprisingly all the quarrels and disturbances were only in the night time while they were alive and after their death also."

"What is that much surprising in it? They have to leave the house in the morning and would be back only in the night. The main problem in that house was Swaroop and he might be available in it only in the night times."

"You are right, I agree with you." Chakravarthy nodded his head. "That Swaroop used to spend most of the time outside even on holidays also."

"Can you say why both of his parents used to quarrel in between themselves so?"

"I could guess by whatever I have heard. And in this case also there was no surprise that they quarrelled only in the night times." There was sudden troubling expression in the face of Chakravarthy. "I think that his father used to force his wife to have sex with him. She has some problems, could not have it with him which resulted in quarrels so. By my understanding with whatever I have heard, this was what would have happened."

"There are guys who want to have sex in their old age also. They just don't worry about the condition of their spouses" with a disgusting expression in his face Anand said.

"None of us do have any animosity towards you people Mr.Anand. In fact we are all feeling so happy as the disturbances from that flat are ceased so after your family's entering into it. But we still remember our experiences." Chakravarthy leaned back in the chair and smiled. "As your family has been residing in that flat quite happily for more than one month without any disturbance, I am thinking whatever may be the problems with it are solved. Slowly and gradually we all also do come into your family and you just relaxed! In no time everything will become quite normal."

"I hope it shall be just so." Swaroop's heart was filled with sudden happiness on hearing that and he got off from the chair he sat. "Now I do go into my home. Anyhow thank you very much for telling me everything like this."

"We are neighbours and we need not thank each other for anything." Chakravarthy also got off from the chair he sat and said. "You just feel happy and enjoy your stay in it. I must say that you have got that flat at a quite lower price and I congratulate you for that."

"Thank you! Don't forget to come to my home." Anand said, turned back and was about to come out of that room but stopped once again hearing the voice of Chakravarthy again.

"I forgot to tell you Mr.Anand. There is small difference to his family members with your family members. There was one additional member in his family but she came into his house only later on after his settling in that house."

Anand once again turned back and looked into the face of Chakravarthy. "Who was she?"

"The sister of his wife and she was a divorcee. She was aged probably twenty two years or so. After coming here, she stayed with that family and went along with them on that day in that car and died with them."

"No Mr.Chakravarthy, it is exactly matching!" Anand paused for a second and his face was reflecting fresh fear. "I took my wife's sister to my home only in the afternoon of this day and she also is aged just twenty two or so. The only difference here is she is a widow. I don't know how long but she is going to stay with my family."

Chakravarthy's face was filled with sudden surprise and shock! "The quarrels have become even more after Swaroop's sister's entry into his house. Swaroop and his wife quarrelled quite intensively about her even I don't know the exact reasons. It was just like she has given fresh start to new set of quarrels between that wife and husband."

There was some eerie silence between them both and after few seconds Anand broke it and said. "Thank you very much for the information Mr.Chakravarthy." Then he turned back once again and went into his flat straight without looking back.

"IS THERE ANYTHING THAT we have to feel anxious in what you have said?" Malathi said after hearing her husband completely at the dinner table. While all of them taking their dinner, it was Malathi who was serving to them then.

"Are not you thinking like that? After Swaroop's family died like that the two tenant families which came into this flat could not stay here for more than a week. But we have been living here for more than one month and we did not experience any discomfort so far." Anand once again paused his eating and asked.

"*Bava* (husband of the sister), it seems......." Saritha laughed and said amidst her consuming the food "..........you are feeling anxious as you people have not faced any trouble like the other residents in this flat before you."

All the others also laughed on hearing that and Anand also laughed. "I am not feeling anxiousness for that but feeling surprise! Why we have been spared, why did not we have been made suffered like the other residents before us in this flat?"

"Wait.............wait.............." Sudarshan who was a listener but not a conservationist till that moment said. ".............your talking appearing quite surprising to me. Why any residents of this flat should suffer whether they are tenants or owners? Instead of thinking in such a way, you are trying to find the ways why we people are not having those odd experiences the previous residents of this flat have."

"Even before answering to that question, tell me one thing. What those odd experiences the previous residents of this flat have? How much unbearable they were to them that they could not cope with even for one week and left this flat?" Thanuja asked him

"I don't know about it just because that Chakravarthy did not tell about their odd experiences to me. What all he said to me was, after that Swaroop's family vacated this flat, two or so families came into this flat on rent but they could not stay in it even for one week." Anand paused few seconds expecting some questions but as no one said anything he said again. "After the death of Swaroop's family that Muchikund's family who are on the left side of us and this Chakravarthy's family who just opposite to us heard quarrelling, weeping yelling of Swaroop's family members from this flat. One noticeable thing here; that Swaroop was not a good guy and all his family members were against him. There were quarrels between the family members. It used to be quite disturbing to the both of our neighbouring families and what even more noticeable here was; they used to hear those things even after the death of Swaroop's family also."

"This information also has been supplied by that Chakravarthy?" Malathi asked him.

"Yes, of course." Anand nodded his head. "I think those tenants also who resided in this flat after the death of Swaroop's family heard those sounds and felt so much panic and left this flat within one week. Because of those incidents, this flat has got very bad reputation. That was the main reason why the owner of this flat sold it such cheaply to us." Anand leaned back in the chair, sighed heavily and completely has forgotten to eat his food.

"Quite good for you people I must say. Otherwise you would not have got this beautiful, big flat at such a huge discount." Saritha said. "Anyhow none of you have been suffering any discomfort after you entered into this place. So please stop worrying about what that Chakravarthy said and start enjoying."

"What you have suggested is indeed quite reasonable and I must appreciate." With an appreciative expression Sulochana said. "But one thing none of the other residents of this apartment are coming into our flat. That is what very much perplexing and troubling to me."

"They heard sounds like that from this flat so they felt too much fear. Even there are no such sounds from here after we entered into this flat, remembering the same they are feeling fear to come into our flat."

"My god! Brother, this is what creating fear in me. Anyhow why they have heard such type of sounds from this flat?" suddenly with lot of fear in her face Thanuja asked him.

"And why they suddenly stopped after we entered into this flat?" Prathap knitted his brows together. "I just cannot say whether it is something to feel happy or sad."

"Auditory hallucination." Saritha once again paused her eating and said. "Swaroop's family sudden death like that created a sort of fear in the residents here especially in the residents of neigh boring flats to this flat. Without their intention they started imagining that they were hearing what they have heard while Swaroop's family was in that that flat. They said the same to the tenants who came into this flat and they also started feeling fear imagining too much. They were just tenants and there would not be much loss to them so left this flat. You people are owners of this flat and you cannot leave this flat as easily as they did. You all people with a resolve to stay in this flat itself without feeling fear to anything. That is the main reason why none of you have any odd experience in this flat."

"How we did forget that we have got a psychology graduate among us?" Malathi laughed and said.

"Anyhow what she has said appears to be the exact reason for the residents here to hear such sounds, the odd experience of the tenants in this flat and why we are not feeling like that. I agree with Saritha's explanation hundred percent." Sudarshan said.

"My strong suggestion for the present is........" before resuming her eating Saritha said. "............just forget about whatever you have heard and start enjoying your lives in this beautiful flat. Slowly and gradually all the other residents of this apartment also come into this flat and you people just don't worry about it."

"Yes, you are right. That was what that Chakravarthy also said. They stop feeling fear and come into our flat sooner or later." After saying that Anand suddenly realised he was not eating and put himself into that.

"IT SEEMS ONCE AGAIN you are thinking about it and worrying." Looking at the moody expression in her husband's face Malathi said. "We all have accepted Saritha's theory and feeling happy. Why cannot you be so?"

They both were on the bed in their bedroom, side by side.

"I just want to accept her theory and relax myself but I cannot. Probing deep I am not thinking that this is such a simple problem. My strong hunch is we did a grave mistake by coming into this flat." Anand said.

"Why you are thinking like that?" suddenly anxiousness filled the face of Malathi and deep frowns gathered on her forehead.

"Just because I do see a strong reason why we have not been made suffered just like the other residents in this flat before us."

"Will you please try to be straight to the point without killing me like this?" Malathi sat straight on the bed and looked straight into his face.

"When entered into this flat, that Swaroop's family also consists six members, his age old parents, himself, his wife, his brother and sister. All of them are of the same age just like us. They are considering our family as their family so they have not been making us suffered as they did to the other residents of this flat."

"You are still not straight." Malathi's face was filled with irritation while she was feeling intensive fear in her heart. "What if there is resemblance like that between our family and that Swaroop's family?"

"I am not very much against spirits and paranormal Malathi. After hearing everything and taking into consideration the present situation, I am thinking that Swaroop's family members are in this flat itself after their death. The continuous uneasy feeling in me also is saying the same thing."

"My god!" Malathi's face was filled with a horrifying expression. "Are you really thinking that it would be so?"

"It is I who purchased this flat. Unnecessarily why do I want to say my decision is wrong?" Anand knitted his brows together.

Malathi did not say anything but picked her lower lip between her teeth-frames and started chewing on that and the fearful expression in her face was just so.

"Why don't you try to say I am wrong? Why don't you say that there are no spirits and only illiterate people do think like that? If you talk like that, I can feel little peaceful."

"I cannot talk like that just because I am not feeling that you are wrong." Malathi released her lip and said. "From the moment I entered into this flat, I also have a strong uneasy feeling insinuating that there are some other people also along with us invisible. I just don't know how the other people are feeling and I don't want to make anyone feel unnecessary fear so I did not say it to anyone."

"I also have such a feeling in me and it started only after we entered into this flat." Anand said. "So there are really some spirits among us invisibly."

"Not any other spirits but that Swaroop and his family." Malathi said. "You are right Anand. They are now among us as spirits. Each one of them seeing themselves in us, I mean Swaroop seeing himself in you, his wife seeing herself in me just like that, so they don't want to trouble us."

"Is there no chance at all that our presumption is wrong? I am a software engineer and I never believed in spirits. Our feeling like this may be just because of some psychological reason and nothing more. The odd experiences of the previous residents of this flat also might be just their imagination. Our neighbouring residents also might be just subjected to auditory hallucination." With a hopeful expression in his face, Anand said.

"I am also a post graduate and I too never believed in spirits till this moment." Malathi smiled. "There is no loss in hoping so. But........." suddenly her face became serious. "............my inner continuous and constant uneasiness and the incidents took place after the death of Swaroop's family are proving that we are not wrong. Unless that Swaroop's family are identifying themselves in each of us, they would not have left us like this"

"What should we do then? Shall we sell this flat and go away?" Anand asked. "I hope we can get more amount than we spent for purchasing this flat. There will be no loss to us."

"No Anand, we are not going to do like that." Malathi once again lied herself on the bed and closed her eyes. "Even we assume that those spirits are among us now, they did not do any harm to us so far. Except the strong uneasy feeling like that, there is no other problem to us. We just continue living in this flat."

"You are absolutely right." Anand also lied himself parallel to her. "We do continue living in this flat. What's the loss even there are some spirits among us if they don't do any harm to us? They were also human beings just like us at one time."

"You are right" Malathi laughed and said without opening her eyes and just in seconds she snap opened her eyes as if something suddenly struck her. "Now there is my sister in this house an additional member un-matching with anyone in that Swaroop's family. What's going to happen to her?"

"I have forgotten to say something to you." Anand also opened his eyes and said. "I just remembered. This also that Chakravarthy said to me. After few days of Swaroop's family settling in this flat, his wife's sister also came into this in almost similar condition of your sister and the age is also just the same. The only difference is she was a divorcee and your sister is a widow. She stayed with Swaroop's family and left with it in the same car on the day of their vacating this flat and died along with them."

"I just don't know what to say and how to take any of this!" once again Malathi's face was filled with horrifying expression.

"After her entering into this flat, the quarrels in the family have become even more especially between that Swaroop and his wife. I need not tell you this also told by that Chakravarthy."

The fear in the face of Malathi was intensified even more by that piece of information but she remained silent as she did not what to say.

"Anyhow there is no necessity to feel fear that your sister will be troubled by those spirits as that Swaroop's sister can see herself in your sister."

"How we can come to an opinion like that? My sister has just come on this day and what if that Swaroop's sister does not want to identify herself with her and trouble her?" Malathi knitted her brows together.

"If it happens so, then itself we think about it. In the meanwhile don't worry yourself with unnecessary thinking. I have to go to office early in the morning and cannot spend the whole night talking with you."

Then Anand closed his eyes forcing himself to sleep and Malathi also did the same but for a long time they could not fall asleep and then also their sleep was with full of nightmares.

Chapter-3

"I am feeling really very much happy that our problem with this flat has been solved after you people settled in this." Parimala was Muchikund's wife and their flat was just beside the flat of Anand and she came into that flat on that Sunday morning at ten when everyone of the Anand's family was in the house itself. "What indeed puzzling to me is how it has been solved by your staying in this!" from the moment she entered into the flat she was talking giving little chance to others to talk.

"That is what we too cannot understand!" while the uneasiness in her was increasing even more Malathi said.

"I believe in coincidences but I must say this is very much!" Parimala's face was brightened once again as she found one other surprising thing to share with them. "It is not just your family members consist just like that Swaroop's family members but ages of your people also just like them! Age old parents, brother and sister, wife and husband without off spring but I can see the only difference is his wife used to have a sister along with them."

"This girl is my sister!" looking at Saritha who sat in a chair little yonder, Parimala said. "She came here just yesterday and she now stays with us for sometime."

Then the shock and surprise that took place in the face of Parimala were abundant. "My god! I just don't know.......I just don't know ....how to understand this! I hope....I hope there should not be similarities in the rest atleast."

"What is that rest, may I know?" even she was feeling fear Parimala felt curious about it.

Saritha, Prathap and Thanuja also came and adjusted themselves on the sofa on which Malathi was then. Anand was in a chair in reasonable distance and he could hear the conversation between Malathi and Parimala comfortably. The only missing two persons were one, Sulochana, who was busy in the kitchen preparing something and Sudarshan who was in his bedroom reading something.

"If you don't know about it yet, it is better that you don't know." With an uneasy expression in her face, Parimala said. "It is not very much good to hear and know about it."

"But we want to know and hear about it." with firmness Malathi said. "Please tell us what it is."

"I used to have lot of intimacy with Swaroop's wife Menaka. We both used to share lot many things in between ourselves. They both wanted children so much but could not have even after three years or so of their marriage. Both of them were upset about that and there were disputes between them. The main dispute started..........." Parimala paused for a second.

"When Swaroop started seeing losses in his business I think." Malathi said in that pause. Anand supplied the whole information he got from Chakravarthi to all his family members.

"No, that too did not make them very much upset and created that much dispute between them." Parimala sighed heavily. "The real dispute between that couple started after Menaka's sister Sirisha entered into their home."

"Why so?" Malathi knitted her brows together but that very piece of information created fresh anxiety not just in her but everyone there who were listening to her.

"That Sirisha was a divorcee. Her husband and in-laws used to torture her a lot and as she could not bear that, she preferred to take divorce. By the time of her divorce, both of her parents were died and what all the relation she has got then was her sister Menaka only so she came here." Parimala paused for a second and her face was with full of uneasiness as if the information she was going to supply was not that much good. "Due to the very much intimacy she has with me, Menaka told me about this also. That Swaroop was indeed a bad guy. Instead of feeling pity on Sirisha's situation, he wanted to take advantage of that. He wanted to have her. On one occasion he went to the extent of raping her also but luckily she could escape."

On hearing that information the expressions in the faces of the people there turned horrific.

"There is a guy Saketh in one of the flats in sixth floor of this apartment. He is a widower and with a son and I don't know how but this Sirisha and that Saketh were acquainted with each other. That acquaintance was developed into intimacy and that intimacy was developed into love. They both wanted to marry also." Parimala was paused with an uneasy expression in her face."

"That is indeed very good! If she marries that guy, it is just like all their problems solved." Malathi said.

"But Swaroop did not agree to that. He was quite against to that alliance."

"Anyone can understand why he is against that alliance. Rascal" Malathi angrily said.

"You are absolutely right. She wanted to have her for himself all the time. That created huge dispute with him in the entire family especially with Menaka.. Poor Sirisha suffered to the maximum here also. She did not study much and did not know where to go as she has no other relatives except her sister."

"Scoundrel! How he could think like that?" it was Anand who said it like that and every one there looked at him. "His wife's sister is just like a sister to him, how he could feel fascination towards her so?"

"Some guys are like that much immoral and unethical! We cannot do anything." Parimala said. "I don't want to startle you people even more but that Sirisha also was pretty even not as much pretty as you and your sister."

That statement would have made those sisters happy at some other time but not then at all.

"Tell, tell us what you more know about that family." Malathi said. "I want to know each and everything of them."

"I have spent enough time here. My husband has plans to go out on this day. I need to give him coffee and breakfast." Parimala said and was about to get off from the chair she sat.

"Oh, please!" Malathi went near to her and made her sit in her chair again. "Just tell us some more about that family. We are all feeling very much curious to hear."

"There is no surprise in you people feeling curiosity like this." Sitting once again in her chair Parimala said and then Malathi came back and slumped in the sofa again. "That Swaroop's sister Neeraja fell in love with a guy Aravind in the flat no.15 in fifth floor and his brother Prathap fell in love with a girl, I still can remember her name Sanjana, in his college. Their love affairs were also created enough problems to Swaroop's family. The most surprising thing was, by the time Swaroop's family left this house in this way and died like that, the alliance between Sirisha and Saketh, the love affairs of his brother and sister were agreed upon and respective families fixed the marriage also."

"Did Swaroop at last agreed to the marriage of his wife's sister with that guy?" Malathi asked.

"All the family members forced him to agree to that, yes he agreed." Nodding her head Parimala said.

"What a family! Brother is in love, sister is in love and sister in law also is in love." With surprise in her face Thanuja said.

"Love affairs have become that common in these days and there is no necessity to feel surprise." Parimala said.

There was some silence ensued and by then Sulochana and Sudarshan also came there and Sulochana settled on the right side of

Malathai on the sofa and Sudarshan dragged an empty chair near to them and slumped himself in it. They both also greeted Parimala with smiles on their lips.

"I am thinking its better that I do go into my house before my husband comes." Once again departing mood came into the face of Parimala and she got off from the chair. "I am sorry if I made you people uneasy by saying any unnecessary things."

"Thank you very much! But please wait. I do go and get you some coffee." Malathi said and got off from the chair with an intention to go into the kitchen and get her some coffee and snacks.

"That is not at all necessary. I took my coffee in my home itself and I don't like to take it again." Parimala's face was filled with an uneasy expression.

"For the first time you came into our house and I don't want you to go without taking anything." Malathi turned back to move away from that place. "Even it is uncomfortable, you must take coffee in our home now."

"Sis, you sit and I go and take that coffee" Malathi was about to move away from that place but before that Saritha got off from the sofa and moved away from that place. Malathi and Parimala both were sat in their respective places again.

"Any other information that you know about that family?" Malathi asked again. "Any little bit of information that you do know about them."

"Why you are this much interested in knowing about them?" Parimala knitted her brows together. "Of course, I know some more but it is even more awkward than the information I shared till now."

"They died like that in an accident and there is a rumour that they are still in this flat itself. No tenant in this flat could stay peacefully even for one week and after they vacated it like that and now we are residing in it. Even the resemblance of our family members with them is quite coincidental, it creates uneasiness in us. We are thinking that Swaroop's family members are identifying themselves in us and left us in peace." Malathi could not think of anything else to make her understand why she wanted all information of Swaroop's family for a reasonable cause. "That is why I wanted to know about everything of that family you know."

"The girl Sanjana, whom this Swaroop's brother loved, came to this home on one day and there was a big quarrel in this home then. She demanded Swaroop's brother Rakesh to marry her but Swaroop did not like that. He wanted to perform his brother's marriage taking huge dowry but Sanjana's family was a poor family. I saw Sanjana went away from this place weeping heavily. Except Swaroop no one else in his family has objection to that marriage."

"We cannot expect anything else except that from such a scoundrel." Malathi angrily said.

"His father also is not a very good character! You know one thing." Parimala lowered her voice considerably. "Despite the point that he is aged sixty five years or so, he used to pester his wife to have sex with him. That woman has been suffering from some problems and could not cooperate with him. What is the surprise if a woman of her age nearing to or more than sixty years suffering from problems and could not participate in sex? Because of that he started an illicit connection with the wife of our watchman Chamanthi. I heard from Menaka that he was going to that woman in the mid-night times."

"My god! Can it be true?" the faces of all the people there filled with horrifying expressions on hearing that and Malathi asked.

"Unless it was hundred percent true, I don't think Menaka would have said that to me." Parimala's face was once again filled with a troubling expression.

There was silence as none of them did not know what to say and after few seconds Parimala herself broke that silence. "I am sorry. I should not have said that." The troubling expression in Parimala's face was intensified even more.

"You need not think like that." Malathi said and by then Saritha came there with coffee cups in a tray not just for Parimala but for everyone else also. "You have shared whatever you came to know and we are all very much thankful to you for that."

After Parimala took her coffee cup from the tray, all the others also did the same and Saritha also slumped on the extreme left side of the sofa with a coffee cup in her hand.

Once again there was silence and Parimala was about to say something but then her husband Muchikund came into that flat.

"It seems you have forgotten me completely." After exchanging greetings with the people there, Muchikund said. "If you throw some coffee in my face, I have to go into the town on an important work."

"Uncle, I give you a cup of coffee just in few seconds." Saritha got off from the sofa along with the coffee cup.

"Please stop. Your uncle doesn't like that coffee being thrown by anyone else except me." With a smile on her lips Parimala said and then she looked into the face of her husband "I really forgot about you engaging in talking with these people. Come, we both go into our flat."

"Saritha, you need not bother about that guest coffee. They both went away." Malathi yelled loudly.

Saritha who went into the kitchen without listening to Parimala and lit the stove again to prepare the coffee, heard that, came there and slumped on the sofa on the left side of her sister forcing Neeraja to give her room. "I missed some piece of information that woman said as I went away to bring coffee. What is that?" Malathi asked her sister.

"My god! Could that be true?" Saritha's face was filled with an awkward expression after she heard about that information from Malathi. "I am not feeling much surprise about that girl's affair. But that Swaroop's father having that illicit affair with that Chamanthi........."

"Once that Menaka herself told about that to this Parimala, we have to believe it." Sighing heavily Malathi said. "Parimala said that they both used to behave lot intimately with each other."

"Anyhow tell me one thing here! Are you thinking that Parimala told us what she really heard from that Menaka are concocted things like that. I know that there people who can get pleasure by concocting false stories so." Neeraja said.

"While I was here I observed her and from her facial expressions and by the way of her talking, I can say that she said only what she really heard but not concocted anything." Saritha said.

"Time and again how and why we forget that we got a psychologist among us!" Anand laughed and said.

"I believe in what Saritha said." Sulochana said. "Anyhow it seems that I have missed large chunk of information she said. What other things she shared with you?"

Then Malathi explained everything that Parimala said to them.

"I don't know what to comment on this but not feeling very well on hearing this." With an uneasy expression in her face Sulochana said. "The similarity of our family has with that Swaroop's family is quite disturbing to me."

"What is in it to be disturbed? That is just coincidence."Sudarshan said.

Anyhow there was such uneasy feeling in everyone of them there and Malathi understood that. "Anyhow I want to know what my psychologist sister is thinking about all of this." As if to make the environment light, Malathi asked her with a smile.

"I absolutely agree with uncle's opinion on this. Our family's similarity with that family is just a coincidence, nothing more." Saritha said. "There are people who can behave nastily like that Swaroop and his father so there is no necessity to think about it. Their ghastly death like that in that accident created a sort of fear in the inmates of this apartment and particularly in the neighbouring flat owners of this flat. Because of that fear they have been subjected to auditory hallucinations and their hearing Swaroop's family's quarrels ever after their death also were just their auditory hallucinations. I have no doubt that this

Parimala said all this including something more to those tenants in this house before us and their odd experiences in our flat also were just hallucinations auditory and visual and I did not feel any surprise in their running away from here. In my firm opinion there is no necessity to feel fear here and there is no chance of any spirits here as there are no spirits in the entire universe."

"What a wonderful explanation really appreciable!" Sudarshan said and there were such expressions in each and everyone there then.

But Saritha could not understand why the uneasy feeling in her became even more even though she believed in what she has said. What she did not know was even there were smiles and happy expressions in the faces of the people there, they were also feeling as much uneasily as she was then.

"JUST GUESS WHAT I HAVE got!"

When Malathi banged into the kitchen and exclaimed like that everyone looked at her. What they could immediately notice was a book in her right hand which she held up. That was another Sunday and they were all again taking their lunch together.

"This is the diary written by that Swaroop's wife. How we have been missed this till now I cannot understand but I found it now while I was cleaning the store room and setting it right."

"Wonderful thing I must say." Neeraja also exclaimed. "Have you read it so far?

"A little only to know that it has been written by her. More than third of this book has been written. Before going through it fully, I just want to share this information to you people. I don't know how the previous tenants of this house missed this book."

"I don't think that they dared to enter into the store room and clean that after hearing all the rumours about this flat." Prathap laughed and said.

"How wide hearted you are I really do appreciate you shared that information without reading it first yourself!" Thanuja said. "Just wait we finish our lunch and we all can together read and know what she has written."

"That is indeed a very better idea! I cannot wait too long to know what she has written." Anand said and fixed himself to finish his lunch as fast as possible.

It was just so to all the other people also there and they finished their lunch as fast as possible and while they were eating the food so Malathi put herself in observing the book postponing taking her lunch later.

"It is a diary okay but she did not write it in a chronological order. She has just written her feelings, incidents that took place in whichever she wanted in this book. At some places her handwriting is good and at some other places it is scraggy indicating that she was worrying and struggling a lot at that time but all her writing was legible."

"In whichever way she has written that, we can come to know lot many things if we read it." Thanuja said.

"Everyone of us is just feeling like that but you know we all cannot read this book at once. If one of us starts reading this book aloud, all of us can know at one time what she has written in it." Anand suggested.

"My friends often tell me that I have sweetest voice. May I read that book aloud then?" Neeraja suggested.

"I have no objection to that and I expect the same from the other people here also." Malathi looked into the faces of the people there while handing over that book to Neeraja and all the others there nodded their heads in agreement.

"I do start from the beginning. She has good handwriting and it is easily understandable!" everyone there started feeling very curious when she started reading that book.

'I am happy! I am absolutely happy! At last we have come to a good place. It is near to Swaroop's office, Rakesh's college also. All the important places are nearby and the environment here also is so nice. How nice if we can own a flat this? If Swaroop starts earning profits in his business, we may hope like that. But I don't expect that he ever can earn profits in his business. It is always in losses and he does not listen to me to close that and start something different.'

"The book started with a happy note" Neeraja paused for a second and looked into the faces of the people there. "Just like in our lives."

"You stop talking and go on with your reading!" feeling irritating Anand said. He did not like her saying like that.

"The neighbours in this floor also are so good. Especially that Parimala. She has become a good friend to me. So much of intimacy was developed between us both and we both have been sharing everything of our lives with each other. She is also worrying as that couple have no children even after ten years of their marriage. She is saying that three years after marriage is not long time and we both can have children. She suggested to me to go to a doctor along with Swaroop for a check up to know if there is any wrong in us both to have children. But I just hate and dislike that rascal! I don't even want to have children from a bastard who wants to have his own sister in law. He is not bothering about her poor condition at all and wanted to have it with her. I just dislike him from the depth of my heart and I want to take divorce from him and go away from here. But I am not educated much and cannot live on my own just like Sirisha and Sirisha also at present completely depended on this family."

Thanuja has to flip the page as that page has come to an end and she need to pause and in that pause Malathi said, "Now I can say whatever that Parimala has said is absolutely true as Menaka herself vouched to the friendship between them both."

"You are absolutely right" Sulochana nodded her head and remained silent as Thanjua once again started reading again.

'I just cannot understand why our are always like this! Swaroop's business is always in losses. As it is not enough Neeraja's love affair with Aravind! They came to our house and quarrelled like that with us. What's wrong in their quarrelling like that? Swaroop's bad reputation is spread all over this apartment and there are always quarrels in this apartment. If it is not so that Aravind's mother sure would have agree to their marriage. I don't know what is going to take place.'

Thanuja gave a little pause before reading again. 'I cannot believe this just I cannot! Here Neeraja's love affair with that guy and there Rakesh's live affair with that girl! Like sister like brother! Swaroop is that much against with his brother's love! He felt happy for his sister's love with Aravind because he could save dowry. But he is absolutely against Rakesh's love with Sanjana as he has to lose dowry. Anyhow I cannot expect Swaroop in good ways in anything at all.'

Thanuja flipped the page as it has come to an end and started reading the matter on the next page.

'I never have expected that girl Sanjana would come to our house like that and create a scene. It appears that they both were deeply in love and I really felt that they both should be married. That girl really was a beauty and I was attracted by her a lot. She said that if her properties have become litigation free her family can become so much rich. But Swaroop is not believing his words and he wants to perform his brother's marriage only with a girl who can give huge salary. I felt very much sorry and pity for that girl but I am helpless. I just hope and pray god that there should come a change in Swaroop and agree to their marriage.'

Once again there was a little pause before Thanuja started reading again.

'I just don't know what to do with Sirisha. She has to divorce her husband and stay at my home in a helpless condition like this and Swaroop is all the time looking for an opportunity to have her. How long I can save her and protect her I cannot understand! How much unfortunate it is that we could not know about that bastard's real nature before her marriage the he, his parents and sister tortured my

Sirisha like that and she has to divorce him! If my parents are alive on this day the situation would have been different but they both also are late. Mom died with heart attack first and dad died in an accused just in one month after her death.'

"Really very much pitiful! Is it is not?" Thanuja paused for a second and asked while flipping that page as the matter on that page has come to an end.

"Really very much pitiful! I am feeling just more and more anger on that bastard Swaroop." Anand said.

Thanuja started reading again.

'I really felt very happy when I came to know that Sirisha and Saketh are in love. If they both married, not just his problem but our Sirisha's problem also would be completely solved. But this scoundrel, it is just as I expected. He is quite against that marriage, he went to his house and quarrelled with him so. He warned him not to talk with Sirisha again. I am afraid the only opportunity to save Saritha from Swaroop and put her life into an order is slipping from our hands."

There were so many things written by Menaka in that diary and they were hearing them carefully while Thanuja reading those to them.

'Losses in Swaroop's business are accumulating day by day. I once again asked him to stop doing that business but he is saying he cannot do that until he pays the money to the customers. I just cannot understand when we can come out of this big lurch.'

'At last, some happy news in our lives! Aravind's mother agreed to his marriage with Neeraja as he is saying that he would commit suicide, if he does not marry her. Anyhow that is good news to our family and one of our burdens will be cleared in an easy way. All of us combining our strength forced Swaroop for Rakesh's marriage with Sanjana and Sirisha's marriage with Saketh. He is more against Sirisha's marriage with Saketh rather than Rakesh's marriage with Sanjana. By this I cannot understand how much he wanted my sister to himself.

I am feeling disgust on myself thinking that I am the wife of such a person.'

'I am afraid that my life is doomed to know only the shocking incidents all the time. My father in law is going to the wife of that watchman for it! The reason he is saying for that is his wife cannot accommodate him whenever he wants it. A sixty five years or so aged man wants sex that much, he goes to another woman if his wife cannot give it to him! Aunty is weeping that she has problems in accommodating him with that. There is no surprise if a sixty years aged woman cannot participate in sex.'

"My god! I just cannot believe what I am hearing." Sudarshan could not remain without exclaiming when Thanuja read that. "He went to the extent to go to watchman's wife at his sixty years of age just because of his wife's inability?"

'That is what I read, did not I?" Thanuja started reading again. 'Now another big shock! Because of his foolish trading, Swaroop has got more than one crore rupees loss. He is saying that we all have to leave this place without any delay. We are all quite against that especially Rakesh, Neeraja and Saritha. But he is saying those creditors would not leave us also if they find us here as we are his relatives. He is saying that we can return to this place very soon again but I don't believe him even a little bit. Anyhow there is no way at all except doing in the way he is asking.'

"This is the last paragraph she has written. After this there is nothing to read in this book." Thanuja closed the book and put that on the table there.

"There is no surprise at all that family has to leave this flat so. I think on that day itself they left this place and she left that diary here. That bastard Swaroop has created such a situation to his family members." Anand said with an angry expression.

"You are right." Malathi nodded her head. "He lost one crore rupees or so of his clients' money in the stock trading. He made them believe that there will be sure profits, traded their money quite unwisely and lost it so. They don't leave his family members also until Swaroop paid that money to them as such all those have to move along with him and died in the accident like that."

"How this diary went into that store room I cannot understand!" Prathap said.

"I think one of those tenants found it in Swaroop's bedroom cupboard, read it and threw it then into the store room. There are some useless things in the storeroom I think belonged to that Swaroop's family." Malathi said.

"But what about the sounds the inmates of this apartment used to hear? And why could not anyone reside peacefully in this flat except us after that Swaroop's family vacated this?" Prathap asked.

"I already gave an explanation to that and I have no objection to say that again." Saritha said.

"Oh, the great psychologist among us is once again ready to give some speech" Malathi said and looked into the face of Saritha with a smile. "We are all very curious to hear even we know that you are going to say the same thing"

"Human mind wants excitement! They feel happiness and thrill in thinking that there are spirits and paranormal creatures around them. Sometimes, even without their knowledge, they start imagining sounds and visuals. These are called as auditory hallucinations and visual hallucinations. Just for the reason I said now, without their knowledge at all, the people here started imagining sounds from this flat. That Swaroop's family vacating this flat in such a way and dying like that was the base for it."

Everyone there laughed except Saritha and Malathi turning her laughter into smile. "I think you have changed your version a little comparing with your previous one. Did you want to give some variety?"

"I remember her previous version and present version also" Sudarshan said who did not laugh with the rest of them and with a serious expression in his face. "And I think both the versions are true. I am also thinking just like Saritha that there is no paranormal in this flat."

"When uncle himself is supporting her like that, I don't think that we have any choice except believe in her two versions." Mocking a serious expression in her face Malathi said. "Moreover I wish it be just like that and I do see no loss in accepting her versions for the present."

Chapter-4

It was two or so in the night and Sudarshan suddenly woke up and his thing was completely up and it needed action. And when he turned his head, he found his wife sleeping peacefully. He went near to her, laid himself on the side of her before putting his right leg across her and kissed on her right cheek.

"My god! What you are doing?" that action of him shocked her amply, she opened her eyes, sat straight and looked into his face with lot of surprise.

"I want it, I want it now." There was full greed in his eyes and face also.

"We have stopped having it together more than twenty years now and you want to have it now?" the shocking expression was just so in her face.

"As my wife it is your responsibility to accommodate me now. If you don't give it to me, to whom I go now to have it?" With an irritating expression in his face, Sudarshan said.

"How shameless you are talking at the age of having grandchildren?" Sulochana angrily said. "You may do that but I cannot. I am feeling shame even to think about that now. Just go, sleep and don't trouble me anymore." Then she laid herself on the bed once again forcing herself to sleep.

Sudarshan then went to his bed, laid himself on it but did not try to sleep. His whole body wanted action and his fully erected thing did not slacken even a little bit. After few seconds he got off from the bed, went near to the table there, opened the draw of it and took his purse from it.

Then he slowly came out of his flat, descended the stairs and went near to the watchman's room. The doors of that room were closed and Sudarshan patted on them rhythmically.

"What do you want sir?" as soon as he opened the doors, Manikyam found him and he asked him surprisingly.

"Don't you know why do I come to your home at this time?" with an irritating expression in his face Sudarshan said. "I want Chamanthi."

"You want Chamanthi? I just don't know what you are talking!" with full of confusion in his face Manikyam said.

"How often I do come here and have it with her? Have you forgotten all that? If you want, I do pay a little more no problem." Sudarshan's face was with full of irritation as if he could not cope with his urge anymore.

"What is happening here?" Chamanthi woke up just then, saw them talking and came near to both of them.

Manikyam explained to her what they both were talking till that moment.

"I make more than the usual payment if you want. I took my purse also with me." Showing his purse to her Sudarshan said. "But I want to have it now itself in the way I want."

"How he knows that he used to come to you for that?" the confusion in the face of Manikyam was just so then also.

"We are not going to bother about it now. He is saying that he would pay even more." Looking at the purse in the hands of Sudarshan with greedy eyes, Chamanthi said. "You just wait patiently outside with our son until everything is finished inside."

Manikyam nodded his head, took his four months' girl baby into his hands and went out of that room. Then Chamanthi took the right arm of Sudarshan into her hands and pulled him into her room. Then she felt so much surprise as Sudarshan was doing as vehemently and forcibly as that Somasundaram, Swaroop's father. It was one positive proof to her that old people also do sex as vigorously as young men. Once it was over with her, Sudarshan dressed himself up and paid two thousand rupees to Chamanthi before coming into his room in the flat again. Then he put that purse in the table drawer again and laid himself on the bed to sleep. Then without much struggle he fell asleep and it was six in the morning by the time he woke up the next day.

"DID I BEHAVE ANY ODDLY with you yesterday night?" when he found Sulochana all alone in the kitchen, Sudarshan went near to her and asked her.

Sulochana stopped the work she was doing at the stove, turned back and looked into the face of Sudarshan with anger in her face. "Instead of feeling shame for the way you have behaved then, you are asking me like this as if you don't remember it at all!"

"Listen....." with irritation in his face Sudarshan said. ".........I remember something vaguely but it is like a dream to me. I got off from my bed and came to you but I just don't remember why I came to you like that then. But I remember you scoffed me off and I don't remember why you did like that. Then I came to my bed again. After that it was just like I went somewhere and did something but everything was just like a dream. I just don't know whether I really did so or it was just my dream."

"You really did it like that. It was not your dream." Now there was surprise in the face of Sulochana. "You came to me for that. You want to have it with me, I did not agree to it and refused vehemently. Then you went back to your bed."

"After a long gap and at this age I wanted to have it with you?" Sudarshan's face was filled with a horrifying expression. "I just don't know what is happening to me."

"Now I believe you. Anyhow you need not feel too much guilty." Putting her right hand on his right shoulder Sulochana said. "Coming to your own wife for that is not a big mistake at whatever age you may be. I just shocked and felt awkward as it was after such a long time."

"That is not the point." With irritation in his face Sudarshan said. "Why I don't remember anything of that in a perfect way? Why that was just like a dream to me?"

"I cannot say anything about that." Without much bothering with what she has heard Sulochana said. In her opinion her husband somehow wanted to have it with her last night and talking like this now only to make her not to get bad opinion on him. It is not wrong that a husband wishing to have it with his wife even at his very old age also and she too need to understand that point. "Anyhow if you want to have it with me next time, I try to cooperate."

Sudarshan did not say anything to that and went away from that place.

"IT WAS HE, I HAVE NO doubt it was he." Chamanthi said to her husband Manikyam while that six months or so of her baby sucking on her right breast. "Otherwise how he can know that I have been providing that? So it is hundred percent true that Swaroop's late family members are in his flat as spirits. That Swaroop's father possessed this man and made him come to me. I have no doubt at all."

"Alright, let it be." Manikyam laughed and said. "We have got our usual income source back."

"But I feel fear thinking that I am being fucked by a devil." There was sudden fear in the face of Chamanthi.

"It is not a devil but a man who fucked you yesterday night and he gave us two thousand rupees also." While looking at the two five hundred rupees notes Manikyam said. They already expended two five hundreds out of the two thousand so far.

"He is possessed by the spirit of that Somasundaram, why cannot you understand?" Chamanthi said with irritation. "If it is not so, how he could ask you straight like that? Could he dare even to think so?"

"You are absolutely right. I agree with you." With a meaningful expression in his face Manikyam said. "What we have to do now?"

Chamanthi picked her lower lip between her teeth-frames and started thinking furiously. After few seconds, she changed that two months or so aged baby to her left breast as that exhausted her right breast, released her lip and said. "Whether it is a devil or man, we are having our money. I accommodate him."

On hearing that, without saying anything more, Manikyam went away from that place as she expected from him.

In fact, it was not just for money for her deciding to have it with him in future also. She did not worry much even her husband was just a lean personality but she worried a lot when he could not keep his thing even for few seconds in hers while doing that. When she expressed her deep regret for him he said, "What I can do? I just cannot manage it long there." Her husband was a relative to her family and she was forced to marry him. His inability in sex came into her notice on the first night itself.

She felt worried but did not get angry on her husband. Even the treatment he has got from some doctors also could not give him the strength to keep his thing more than those few seconds not to say moving it furiously and giving her the pleasure. While she was burning with desire and worrying too much on one day he said. "I can understand your suffering. I have no objection if you want to satisfy yourself with someone. If it helps financially also to us, it would be even more good."

It was by that time Manikyam joined in this apartment as watchman and that all has taken place in the raw days of their marriage. After hearing her husband so, Chamanthi was on the lookout for a suitable guy to get her urge satisfied! As it was like that, Manikyam suddenly became ill and they needed money. On that day she went to the Secretary, Mangal Rao, and asked him for some financial help. At that time, Somasundaram also was with him in his house.

"I already gave five thousand rupees loan to your husband and that has not been cleared yet. Until that loan is cleared; I cannot give you anything more." Mangal Rao curtly said and she came back into her room with a crestfallen face. Once entered into the room, she was about to close the door of it but she saw Somasundaram at the threshold. It was just like he followed her there without her knowledge.

"I can help you with the money you want." There was troubling expression in his face and she almost understood why it was so.

"We want two thousand rupees............" with a meaningful expression in her face, she said. "..............but I cannot say when we can repay that."

"If you do me a little favour, you need not repay it at all." The troubling expression in his face was disappeared and now there was a smile on his face as if he understood her consent.

"After eleven in the night. Just tap on the doors and that is enough." Suddenly her voice became firm. "I should have my money first before anything happens."

He nodded his head, went away from that place and it was twelve or so in the night by the time he has come. She felt little guilty when he gave her two thousand rupees in the beginning itself. She felt even more guilty while he was getting on the top of her on the bed after her husband went away from that place. However much she was longing for sex, however much they were in financial need, it was very first time to her to have another person on the top of her to do that.

What surprised her a lot was the vehemence with which he did that and the way he had it with her! It was not at all expected from a sixty plus aged guy. He made her absolutely naked and made himself so and there was no place in her body that he did not touch and kiss! The back side of her left ear was his favourite place and she did not remember how many times he kissed there, licked there and has bitten slightly.

Inserting his thing into her was also with ease and convenience, here also there was another shock and surprise for her! It was like infinite and she felt eternal pleasure while he was moving his bulged penis between her tightly closed vaginal lips. She just did not know that a man could do it that long and could not remain without yelling when he discharged into her with force. When he slumped on the top of her like an emptied sack, she tightened her hug around him, kissed on his head and said. "I never knew that a man can do it this much to a woman." She did not know whether her remark so made him happy or not.

"May I come here like this occasionally for it? My wife doesn't agree to give it to me every now and then." He asked her after getting off from the bed and dressing himself up completely.

"How unfortunate of her!" she also got off from the bed and started dressing herself. "Not just for the money but the pleasure of it also, I always welcome you like this."

He nodded his head and went away from that place and in a discreet and secret way that was continued until that family went out in that car and died like that. As sexually and financially also that man was enough, Chamanthi did not try to have another man as long as she has it with him.

Even though she managed to open and maintain relations with some other men in that apartment for satisfying her financial assistance and sexual urge also afterwards, she really felt when she lost Somasundaram so. She felt more for the loss of his vigorous fucking rather than for the loss of the amount even it was always little more than the others.

Now, for the present situation, she did not know whether to feel happy or sorrow! The same vigorous fucking, the same enjoyment with the same aged person! How it was possible unless that Somasundaram really died, became a spirit and possessed this man? This man would not have dared even to think to come and ask her like that if he has not been possessed by Somasundaram's spirit. However much enjoyable it was to her, it was indeed creepy to think that she was being fucked by a man possessed by a devil.

SARITHA WAS ALL ALONE in her room with her own disturbing thoughts. Even the thoughts were disturbing to her now, the present situation was quite better comparing with the situation of her past. In those days the thoughts used to torture her not just disturbing. She suspected she could not have much enjoyment with Nandagiri before her marriage itself considering his lean and short figure but agreed for marriage with him as she was as much desperate as her step-mother to go away from her as she wanted to get rid of her. What all she wanted was atleast nice treatment in his hands and in the hands of her in-laws. But that also has been proved absolutely against her wish. The mother and sister of her husband systematically tortured her and they used to get sadistic pleasure in doing so. Her husband Nandagiri was a heavy drinker and his concentration was always on drinking and he did not stop his drinking habit even his both lungs were absolutely damaged because of that and just in six months or so of her marriage he died. His death like that did not affect Saritha at all and indeed she felt happy but the torture in the hands of her mother in law and sister in law has become maximum and it has become that much unbearable she wanted to go to her step-mother's home but she has given a stern warning not to step into her home again. In the beginning she did not want to trouble her sister by entering into her home even her sister invited her but as she could not bear anymore the torture in the hands of her in laws she has taken the decision to come to her sister's come and now she was here itself. As her in-laws also just wanted to get rid of her they did not object her going out from their home and coming and staying in the house of her sister was indeed a big relief to Saritha.

But what about the relief of her body? It was quite surprising to her even while she was being tortured by her in-laws in their home her body used to crave for it a lot. Her husband's trying and failing in doing that just made the urge in her trebled. Once she settled in the house of her sister and relaxed like this just making the continuing urge in her even more and more. How much, how much she wanted to have it with someone? How nice it would have been if she got married with someone and could have it regularly with him?

She sighed heavily, went near to the bed and laid herself on that horizontally face down on the bed while pressing her chest strongly to the bed and face to the pillow while widening her legs to the maximum. Whenever she felt uncontrollable sexual urge, she would do like that and it gave her little comfort. She sighed heavily, opened her eyes and then she found the paper back from Parimala's home. That Parimala has a habit of reading fiction and Saritha also sometimes read fiction. Suddenly she wanted to read that fiction, sat straight on the bed and started reading it.

In the beginning that book was not much interesting in her but after reading some pagers she felt it was really interesting and she was just went on reading it like that.

"IT WOULD HAVE BEEN quite nice on this day if that aunty with us." Saketh said with his two years aged son, Anurag, looking into his face. "She used to look after you that well! I never need to worry about you once I went to bank. Now a day I am feeling very much to leave you in that baby care centre to go to the bank."

Saketh has been working as a manager in a reputed private sector bank, he bought this flat just two years back and settled himself. He has other properties also along with this flat and financially he has no problems. His marriage was over after he settled in this flat and he was so happy with his wife and they both have got a son also. But quite unfortunately, when Anurag was just one month or so aged, Saketh's wife died in an accident. He worried more how to look after his son rather than for the loss of his wife so.

But, at that time, Sirisha, the divorcee in the flat no.3 in the second floor of this apartment, got acquaintance with him, that acquaintance developed into friendship and she started looking after Anurag. Before she started looking after Anurag, Saketh has to leave him in a baby care centre. It was just like Anurag's problem was solved for him forever. They have plans to marry and became man and wife as it was quite convenient and comfortable thing to both of them. One big problem was, that Swaroop, the husband of her sister did not want her to marry Saketh and he came and quarrelled with him also on one occasion and threatened him not to talk with Sirisha again. Anyhow the other family members of him forced him to agree with the marriage of Sirisha with Saketh and Saketh thought everything was alright.

But shocking him and making him completely despaired that Sirisha left this flat suddenly on that day along with that family and died in that car accident. It was indeed very much difficult to him to believe now also. How bad luck haunting him like that every time he could not understand! Because of his good job, his properties and handsome personality, women are ready to marry him but he was not at all ready to marry anyone. He was in real love with that Sirisha and he could not think about anyone else in his life. So once again he preferred to leave Saketh in that baby care centre while he could not attend on him but did not prefer to marry again.

So far in this one year or so after Sirisha's death like that, he has accustomed to a routine. There was a servant maid to him who would come everyday and do the household work and he himself look after most of the work of Anurag as he has happiness in doing that. Once the work in the home was over, he would leave Anurag in the nearby baby care centre and then to his bank and while coming back from the bank he took his son along with him. Every day he has been doing like this for the last one year or so and on this day he did not know why but his mind was full of Sirisha's thoughts. While his mind was occupied with the thoughts of Sirisha, he heard calling bell sound, went near to the doors and opened them wide. There at the threshold stood Saritha with a smile on her face. On one or two occasions Saketh saw her, to be frank attracted by her beautiful figure also but did not know in which flat she was residing.

"So you all ready to go to the bank." Saritha said continuing the same smile on her lips. "You prepared your son also in the best way possible."

"Excuse me, I don't know who you are and why you have come here!" With surprise and shock in his face, Saketh said.

"I agree that I have gone away from you rather sudden like that on that day. And it is my mistake I did not contact you even for once all these days." With gathered frowns on her forehead Saritha said. "But I have my own reasons for doing like that. It is not because I have no love for you both. So, please stop treating me like a stranger and let me come in."

Saketh did not know what to do when she came straight into his flat, went near to Anurag and took him into her hands and kissed on his right cheek. "I hope atleast you do forgive me for the mistake I did."

Then Anurag laughed loudly, put his both hands around her neck and kissed on her left cheek. That action of Anurag made Saketh very much surprise! Anurag has got such nature he would not go easily to anyone and accept them.

"Just see! Your son has no anger on me and he excused me. Why cannot you follow his suit?" still holding Anurag in her hands and hugging him close, Saritha asked while looking into the face of Saketh.

"Madam, please." Saketh took Anurag from her with force and made him stand on the floor there. "I don't know who you are and I never like strangers behave like this with me and my son. If you please go away from here, I have to drop my child in the baby care centre and go to my bank."

That action of him, taking his son forcibly like that from her, was just like rattled something in her and she came to her full consciousness.

"Where I am now? What I am doing here?" with lot of confusion in her face, looking at the four sides of that house, Saritha said.

"You are in flat no.14, fourth floor, Madhurima Apartments. Is that information enough for you?" with lot of irritation in his face Saketh said. "You came here all by yourself and now talking like this? I just cannot understand what type of game this is!"

"I have to be in flat no.3, second floor." Her face was filled with a horrifying expression. "I just cannot understand what I have to do in this flat!"

"Just a moment!" Saketh was once again shocked on hearing that. That was the flat in which Sirisha used to live with her brother in law, sister and the rest. He knew about the rumours but did not believe them at all. He was little puzzled when he came to know that the tenants who came into that flat could not reside more than a week in it. He knew that for a long time that flat was fell vacant and only now through this girl came to know that it was occupied again. He just did not prefer to go towards that flat after his Sirisha died like that. "You are residing in flat no.3?"

"Of course, yes!" Saritha nodded her head. "My *bava* purchased the same and I am now living along with his family."

"Who else are living with you now in that flat?" still feeling lot of surprise Saketh asked her.

"My *bava,* his wife, his parents and his brother and sister." Saritha answered to him still with a confusing expression in her face. "I am absolutely sorry that I bothered you in this way. I really cannot understand why I came like this into your flat. I was reading some fiction book in my bedroom in my flat and it was just like suddenly something entered into me and made me come here like this. It is all just like a dream to me and I knew that I was talking something with you but did not know what I was talking. What I have talked with you?"

"Never mind. You did not talk anything wrong." By then Saketh perfectly understood why that woman came into his flat like that. "You just asked how my son and I am doing now." He conveniently lied to her.

"But you are a complete stranger to me! Why should I come into your flat and ask like that?" the surprise in her face has become even more.

"I too cannot say anything about it. But surprising things like that sometimes do happen." Once he realised the reason behind her behaviour so, he started feeling towards her just he felt towards Sirisha. To be frank Saritha was more beautiful and cute than Sirisha also even that would not be mattered much to him.

"I am sorry. It seems that I detained you both." It was just like she realised that only then. "I go now into my flat and I am once again extremely sorry for the inconvenience I caused to you."

"It is not at all so. Your acquaintance has given me and my son only happiness." The smile then on his face was just because of his absolute joy in his heart. He did not know how but he was feeling just like his Sirisha entered into his house then "Come like this now and then and that indeed would give happiness to us both."

"I don't know what to say to this." She turned back. "I am going now." Then without saying anymore she came away from that place fast.

"I JUST DON'T KNOW WHY I have behaved like that, I just don't know." Saritha banged the dining table there with both of her hands and at that time Saritha, Thanuja, Malathi and Sulochana were in the kitchen. "I just cannot understand why I behaved like that!"

"Why don't you say it is something.....something....a trick of your mind?" Thanuja laughed and said. "You are a psychology graduate, have you forgotten about it?"

"Of course, I did not." Saritha slumped in one of the chairs at the dining table and said. "But I must say that I never have thought that once person's mind can make him or her to behave like this! I just don't with what name this disorder should have been called!"

Malathi was hearing her sister silently and if she did not come to know about Swaroop's sister also through Anand, she would have enjoyed that just like Sulochana. So far Anand and she understood why Swaroop and his family members left them without troubling them at all. There was no doubt that Swaroop's sister was identifying herself with Saritha and has chosen to possess her body temporarily. What they should do if the other family members of Swaroop also took such a decision?

"Don't think about this much for the present." Malathi said forcing a smile onto her lips. "Even psychologists and psychiatrists' minds also are not immune to hallucinations and imaginations............"

"Sis, you did not get the point right." Saritha said interrupting her vehemently. "This is not just hallucination or imagination! I went there like that without my intention and behaved like that with him. It is just like a dream to me. It was just like I was possessed........"

"Possessed by whom? Can you be specific? I think it is the sister of that Swaroop. Even you don't like I want to say there is lot similarity between you both and she was in love with that Saketh............."

"Will you stop talking nonsense like that?" interrupting Saritha with a loud voice Saritha said. "I never do believe in such type of nonsense."

"I too not ordinarily. But just see and try to analyse. Just because of your non-believing in them spirits don't become non-existent. If it is not so a girl psychologically and physically healthy would behave like that?" Thanuja knitted her brows together.

"You have to think Saritha getting irritation does not solve the problem." Sulochana said. "It is really very much surprising a girl who is quite opposite to spirits and paranormal is possessed by a spirit!"

"But aunty you know.........." Saritha was about to say something.

"Alright, alright......" this time Malathi interrupted her while the chill feeling in her heart was increasing even more. ".............whatever it may be, don't worry about it for the present and just try to be peaceful."

"Anyhow do you remember what you have talked with him and how you have behaved there?" Sulochana asked Saritha as if she did not listen what Malathi said.

"No, it was all just like a dream and quite vague." Once again Saritha's face was with full of confusion. "I talked something but I don't remember exactly what I talked! I did not know how it happened but I suddenly came into my full sense. You just cannot understand how much ashamed I felt at that person."

Then Sulochana remembered what her husband Sudarshan talked with her. If Saritha has an experience like that, there was no surprise that her husband also faced similar situation. The big question was why they were subjected to such hallucinations? As it was supposed by Thanuja that Saritha was possessed by Swaroop's sister, her husband was possessed by Swaroop's father.

"I am feeling fear that I suddenly subjected to a psychological disease. Unless it is so........." Saritha tried to say something more after few seconds' silence.

"For the present I want to give you the same suggestion that Malathi gave. Don't worry about the weird experience you have so far. If you feel like that again in future, we do think about what to do." Thanuja interrupted her and suggested.

"On thinking deep......" Saritha sighed heavily and said. "........what you have suggested now is reasonable to follow."

"I JUST DON'T KNOW HOW to take any of this." After explaining Saritha's experience to Anand, Malathi said. "What you are thinking now?"

"It is clear to both of us now, don't you see?" sitting straight on the bed Anand said. "That Swaroop's sister is in this flat along with us and as she is in love with that Saketh she went to him possessing our Saritha like that."

"You are absolutely right Anand." Malathi also sat straight opposite to Anand and said. "Whatever her name may be I don't remember now, that woman Swaroop's sister wanted to interact with her lover, she possessed our Saritha and made her go to him like that and talked to him through her."

"Absolutely it is just like that." Nodding his head in agreement, Anand said.

"It has become clear to us now that they just don't stay along with us but possess us also. What happens if the other spirits here also start possessing us with the respective person matching to them?" Malathi knitted her brows together.

"Very difficult thing to answer." With a troubling expression in his face Anand said. "But we cannot deny such possibility."

"But I am thinking Anand, whatever you may say............" suddenly there came a troubling expression into the face of Malathi also. "...........it is quite better that we may vacate this house and go somewhere else."

"It is not as easy as you are thinking." Anand said. "First thing we cannot give this house on rent to anyone just because the spirits in this house except us don't let anyone stay here peacefully. Next thing, we have to pay huge amount as rent if we change ourselves into some other comfortable accommodation. Don't forget my present salary is not much because of the EMI I have to pay every month on the loan I have taken for purchasing this house."

"I also do a job. Don't forget that I am a post graduate in English literature."

"I never forget that. This is something we sure can consider." Anand laughed. "But you have no experience in any field. No one feels too much enthusiastic to take inexperienced candidates even they are post-graduates. Even you can manage to get a job, we cannot say where you do get it and there are certainly some problems if we both are engaged in jobs now."

"Oh, don't talk like that! I sure can get some job nearby. It is not that much difficult thing to do if I really try. There may be companies and offices which may take inexperienced post graduates also but with lower salary" Malathi said. "Moreover your dad also helps us financially if there is necessity."

"Alright, you too try for a job and we do as you suggested after your getting a job." Once again nodding his head Anand said. "But first thing we have to explain this to the other family members. They all are very much happy in this house now and feel very much worried on hearing this. Moreover......." he paused for a second before saying "..........we have to continue in this house until you get some job nearby and we are financially comfortable to take some other house on rent."

"You are right." Malathi nodded her head in agreement.

"Anyhow we have to agree with something here." Anand said. "So far those spirits did not do any harm to us. That spirit also did not do any harm to your sister but possessed her and made her to go to that gentleman and talk with him. We are just assuming that other spirits also may possess us but it may not happen like that at all. Why don't we feel unnecessary fear like this?"

"Once again you are right!" Malathi smiled. "But it is indeed very much weird to think that we are living along with spirits."

"Of course, I agree!" Anand nodded his head "But presently we don't have any other option."

Then Malathi did not stop him at all while he was gaining onto her. She cooperated with him in the way he wanted and became an active participant also in that sexual intercourse thinking all the time how much nice it would have been if she became pregnant. It was more than three years that they were married and having no children so far was the most worrying thing to both of them.

Chapter-5

"Why do you stand like that looking into my face as if I am stranger?" while Sanjana was looking into the face of Prathap with surprise and shock, Prathap said. "Why you are trying to avoid me and going away every time? Why you are maintaining distance like this from me, I cannot understand!"

Sanjana was in the playing ground then and when she was all alone Prathap came there and started talking with her looking into her face.

"I just cannot understand what you are talking! You are an absolute stranger to me." With the same surprise and shock in her face, Sanjana said.

"You are calling me as a stranger? You are calling your Rocks as a stranger?" this time there was shock in the face of Prathap also. "If you don't want to marry me and don't want to talk with me say it just so but don't behave that you do never know me."

"My Rocks! What the bloody hell you are talking? My Rocks died one year or so back! If you try to harass me like this again I give a complaint against you to the police." After saying so, Sanjna tried to move away from that place but Prathap blocked her way.

"What you are saying I just cannot understand! I am in the same flat now also and looking forward so eagerly for our marriage. It is you who are trying to avoid me for the reason best known only to you." Prathap also angrily said still blocking her way.

"Rascal, if you don't let me go now, I do what I said." Throwing him back with both of her hands forcibly and moving away from that place Sanjana said.

"Just a moment please, just few seconds of your time." When Prathap said that with absolute change in his voice, she turned and looked into his face.

"Did I behave awkwardly with you? Did I talk anything offensively with you? If it is so, I am absolutely sorry for that."

"That means you don't know what you have talked with me till this moment?" Sanjana knitted her brows together while observing the expression in his face which was appearing quite genuine.

"Absolutely just like that, I must say." Nodding his head in negation Prathap said. "It is just like that someone possessed me and made me talk so. I knew that I was talking with you but I did not know what I have talked with you. If you don't mind, please tell me what I have talked with you?" with a pleading expression in his face Prathap asked her.

"You said that you are my Rocks. I was in love with that guy and marriage has been settled between us both also. I am so happy but he suddenly died in a car accident along with his family. I just cannot understand why did you come to me and talk pretending like my Rocks." Once again there was surprising expression in the face of Sanjana. To her Prathap was appearing like a good boy and would not do pranks.

"I did not pretend and I did not just know why I behaved like that with you. Please believe me." Prathap's face was with full of hurt. "Where was that Rocks used to live?"

"His real name is Rakesh and I used to call him Rocks." Then she told him about the place where he used to live. "I went to his home also. But on one day that his whole family died in a car accident along with him making my heart shattered into hundred pieces. There is no happiness to me from that moment and I just cannot remain without thinking about my Rocks always" Suddenly there was a pathetic expression in her face.

"I don't know how to say this and what to talk!" there was abundant shock in the face of Prathap then. "But I am now living in that very flat!"

"I just cannot understand what you are talking!" with a confusing expression in her face Sanjana said. "What it is that you are living in that flat now?"

"Yes, my brother purchased it. I am living in that flat along with my brother, sister in law, sister and my parents."

"Rakesh also used to live in that flat with his brother, sister in law, sister and his parents." Frowns gathered on the forehead of Sanjana.

"Yes, I know about that. I came to know from the inmates there that Swaroop's family has the members just like us. That Swaroop used to live in that flat along with his wife, parents, sister and your lover Rakesh." Prathap sighed heavily. "But for quite sometime I have been feeling quite uneasily, just like someone else also in me besides myself. I just cannot understand why I have behaved like this with you. I think I need some psychological help."

Sanjana took her lower lip between her teeth-frames and started chewing on it while the deeply gathered frowns on her forehead were insinuating the consternation in her.

"It is not just me in fact. My vadina's sister also behaved as if she was possessed by that Swaroop's sister. She went to the lover of Swaroop's sister who is also living in our apartment and talked with him just like her. In fact my vadina's sister is a psychologist and she is not believing that she has been possessed by a spirit. I also just want to think like that but cannot understand how to take two people behaving so."

On hearing that Sanjana's face was filled with shock and surprise and her forehead was creased with deep frowns.

"I am absolutely sorry that I made you upset like this. I try to find out a solution to this problem. I do go now." Prathap turned back and took two steps.

"Just a moment please!" he turned back and looked into her face when he heard her voice with lot of imploring in it.

"Can we both go to canteen and have some coffee?" with an imploring expression in her face also, Sanjana said. "I just want to have some talking with you."

AT THAT TIME THE CANTEEN in that college was almost empty and they both chose a table in the corner and ordered coffee.

"What do you really want to say miss?" frowns gathered on the forehead of Prathap and there was confusing expression in his face.

"I know about my Rocks fully and absolutely. He just cannot forget me as I cannot forget him forever. He fought tooth and nail with his brother and made him agree to our marriage. But it was just quite unfortunate that he died like that along with his family in that car accident." She sighed heavily. "After hearing like this I can understand only one thing! He and his family members are in that flat as spirits waiting for someone matching with them to possess them to contact their loved ones. I cannot say about your sister but you are just like my Rakesh! The same height, the same width and the same face cut with the same age and studying in the same class! And it is convenient to my Rocks to interact with me by possessing you. Whatever you may say I just believe that it is my Rocks who talked to me like that." In the end she cupped her face with both of her hands and broke out into weeping. "Oh, Rocks! Now you are a spirit!"

"Oh, please, don't weep. It is not good if people observe you like this!" Rakesh hurriedly said as the waiter also has come there with coffee cups.

"I am absolutely sorry." Sanjana hurriedly wiped her tears with her right and becoming normal said.

Waiter put the coffee cups before them both and went away from that place as if he did not observe anything there.

"I know that family was financially in huge troubles. They wanted to go faraway out of the reach to their creditors for sometime and left that flat in a car but it happened like that. If all our properties were not in court litigations then, I sure would have helped them and it would not have happened like that. Now we have got all our properties and I am a very rich girl! But what is the use?" Once again there was a deep worrying expression in her face.

"We got hold of the diary written by Rakesh's vadina. She has written many a thing in that diary and yes, you are right! To escape from their creditors, they left that place like that on that day." And she heard with a horrifying expression in her face while he was explaining what they came to know through the diary. He did not leave anything and she listened everything he said with the same attention .

"That Swaroop was indeed a bad guy and I don't feel sorry for his dying like that." When Prathap was over with his saying, Sanjana said. "I pleaded to him a lot to agree with our marriage but he did not agree. I said we sure do get our properties back soon and once we got back our properties I help them but he did not believe in me. Anyhow all his family members made him agree to our marriage but it has happened like that."

"I think that his family members have convinced him that you sure would get your properties otherwise he would not have agreed to both of your marriage. He is really a very bad guy."

"You are right. Unless he is such a bad man, he did not want to have his own sister in law. He opposed her marriage also with the guy she loved, Rocks told me." With an angry expression in her face Sanjana said. "He deserved a death like that but not his other family members."

"Certainly not his other family members! The marriages of his sister and sister of his vadina also were settled with their respective lovers and they were so happy but just because of that Swaroop they had to leave like that and die like that! With his foolish ideas, he put his whole business into deep losses and indebted to his creditors that much." Rakesh said angrily.

There was some silence between them both as if both of them did not know what to say and breaking that silence Sanjana suddenly said. "Can I make a small request to you now?"

"Of course, you can." Rakesh smiled and said.

"May I come to your home? I just want to see whether I can feel the presence of Rakesh there." There was a pleading expression in her face.

"Whenever you want, I have no objection." Prathap said continuing the same smile. "Just tell me when do you want to come?"

"Tomorrow evening. Tell your family members about this."

"I do that. We both go together from here tomorrow evening." Prathap said. "If you don't mind we both may go to our class now. We have spent enough time outside."

Sanjana nodded her head, got off from her chair and walked away from that place. Prathap also did the same. As neither of them has preferred to touch, the coffee in the cups on the table was remained full and became cold.

"I JUST CANNOT UNDERSTAND why it is happening like this in our lives." After hearing everything clearly along with others Saritha exclaimed. "First me and next you! How we have to take this?"

It was night time and they were all taking their supper in the dining hall.

"We have to take this in a simple way that each of the spirits of Swaroop's family are preferring to possess the family members of us matching with their age and gender and are trying to fulfil their wishes. That Swaroop's sister in law Sirisha is just of the age of you so she preferred to possess you and make you to go to that Saketh and talk like that. In fact it was that Sirisha who went to that Saketh and talked with him on that day possessing your body. On this day that Rakesh,

Swaroop's brother, preferred to possess our Prathap, went to that Sanjana and behaved like that. I cannot give any other explanation than this to it." Malathi said.

"Absurd! Absolutely absurd! I don't believe in these spirits and paranormal." Saritha vehemently said.

"Then you give some plausible explanation for your both behaviour." Sulochana said.

"For the present I just cannot! I cannot understand anything." Suddenly there was a helpless expression in the face of Saritha.

"In the absence of any other reasonable explanation to this, we may better agree with what Malathi has said." Sulochana said.

"If what Malathi has said is true, what we have to do if the other family members of that Swaroop's family choose our remaining family members matching with their age and gender and try to fulfil their wishes?" Sudarshan asked.

"Not just that, there is no guarantee that Saritha and Prathap are not going to be possessed by Swaroop's sister in law and brother again. What type of things they may make them to do next time, we cannot say. What the other family members of Swaroop make the rest of us to do if they possess us also we cannot say" Thanuja said with a horrifying expression in her face.

"What if we leave this house and go away." Prathap suggested. "I am feeling very much eerie to stay in a house where there are more than one spirit and they possess us also."

"You try to remember one thing here brother." Thanuja said. "We have to clear the huge loan we took for purchasing this house and it becomes simply difficult to us if we take some other house on rent somewhere else. Moreover we cannot give this house on rent considering the status of it at present. I don't think we get the price back if we put this flat on sale now however much low it is just because of the bad reputation of this flat now."

"Even it is full of spirits, I don't like to sell it back." Anand said with firmness. "Except possessing two of our family members, those spirits did not do any harm to us. In fact I cannot even know the presence of them except some uneasy feeling in me."

"After our hearing weird things, some uneasiness entered into our mind and stayed there. That need not be taken into consideration at all." Saritha said. "Still I am opposing to the idea that there are spirits in this flat. Even though I was also has such experience, the odd behaviour of Prathap and I is some sort of psychological disorder. Trying to sell this flat with that fear is just foolishness."

"For the first time I do like my sister wholeheartedly. Whatever may be our experiences in this house, I just don't want to lose it. This house is in a very convenient place and we cannot get some other house like this, if we lose it." Malathi said.

"One other thing *Vadina* (brother's sister)" Thanuja said. "Even we do agree that there are spirits in this flat, why should we think that they do harm to us? Before dying they were also human beings just like us. Moreover, except that Swaroop, all the other family members of him are good."

"This is also true." Malathi nodded her head.

"Then we are all unanimous in our opinion not to sell this house." Anand looked into the faces of the other people.

"Yes, of course." Sudarshan nodded his head and said and there were such expressions from other people also.

Sulochana looked at her husband with an odd expression in her face. She saw him going out of the flat in the middle of the night on one or two occasions and she perfectly could understand where he was going. If he has not been possessed by that Swaroop's father, he would not have gone like that for it. She just could not dare to affront a person possessed by a spirit to stop him.

"Anyhow, I already told you people that Sanjana would come to this house on tomorrow evening." Prathap reminded them.

"We all gave our agreement then itself. If coming to this flat would give some peace to that tormented soul, we all feel happy." Malathi said.

It took more than usual time to them to finish their supper as they finished it all the time talking in themselves.

"WHY YOU ARE LOOKING into my face as if you don't remember me at all? I am your Neeraja, your lover and we are going to be married very soon." looking into the face of Aravind, Thanuja asked him. "What happened to you may I know?"

"Nothing happens to me, I am alright." Aravind said with a surprising expression in his face. "I know that you are now residing in the flat where my Neeraja used to reside. But I just don't know why you are thinking yourself as Neeraja and talking like this."

"Used to reside? I am always residing there." Thanuja angrily said. "If you fell in love with another girl and don't want to marry me, tell that straight. But don't talk in this way."

"What you both are talking here?" Aravind's mother Manorama came there and asked them while looking into the face of Thanuja with surprise.

Aravind told his mother what that Thanuja said to him then.

"I saw this girl in this apartment but I don't know that she is residing in that flat now." Manorama said with surprise! "For a long time that flat fell vacant as no one wants to come and reside in it as the rumours are so."

"Yes, she is residing in that flat with her family members now, I saw her coming out of that flat on one or two occasions. Whether those people purchased it or in it on rent I cannot say. But I don't know why she is talking like Neeraja." Aravind said with a confusing expression in her face. Even after the death of his lover Neeraja in that car accident like that, Aravind as often as possible went to that flat and look at that however much painful it was but he did not hear any voices of that Swaroop's family from it. While he was thinking that it was just a rumour saying that Swaroop's family members in it, it happened like this on this day.

"She is appearing like a decent girl and just like that Neeraja! What is the necessity to her to behave like this!" Sulochana went near to Thanuja, put her both hands on her shoulders and shook them while looking into her face straight. "Now tell me who you are and why you are here?"

Instantly there was a startling expression in the face of Thanuja and it was just like she has come to her senses only then. "Whose flat is this and why I am here?"

"This is our flat and it is you who need to answer this question." Aravind laughed and said. "Why did you come here and whom do you want?"

"I just don't know......I just cannot remember anything!" with absolute confusing expression in her face Thanuja said. "It is all just like a dream to me. I knew that I have been coming to you but I did not know why I have come like that! I knew that I was talking with you but did not know what I talked. I am absolutely sorry if I behaved or talked offensively with you people."

"You did not talk anything offensively but you said you are my Neeraja. Neeraja used to reside in the house in which you are residing now. We both were engaged and were going to be married but that family suddenly died in a car accident." While saying that a pathetic expression filled the face of Aravind.

"Of course I know about it." With shocking expression in her face, Thanuja said. " But I just cannot understand why I behaved like this coming into this flat."

"Don't break your head thinking about it." Sulochana said. "Just relax yourself in this chair and I get you some coffee. After taking coffee, you become fully normal again."

"No, aunty, I don't want. I just want to go into my flat now." Thanuja said and turned back.

"Just stop. I will drop you in your flat now."

"My flat is in this apartment itself and I can go myself there." Thanuja smiled and said while taking steps. "You need not take trouble at all."

"No, I want to come to your flat to introduce myself also. It is indeed necessary to know about all the inmates of this apartment and I am feeling sorry I did not do that yet." Sulochana said, reached her and put her right hand around her shoulders.

After that Thanuja and Manorama moved away from that place and Aravind slumped himself in the chair there sighing heavily in himself.

"THERE ARE WEIRD HAPPENINGS after we entered into this flat." After hearing what Manorama said to her, Malathi said with full anxiousness in her face. "It is not just our Thanuja, her brother Prathap and my sister Saritha also behaved like that." Then Malathi explained to Manorama about their odd behaviour while she was listening with rapt attention "But we cannot blame anyone! We knew this flat is haunted before our purchase of this itself. At that time we did not believe in spirits at all and purchased this flat as it was coming at such a lower place. I just cannot understand how to take the present happening like this." In the end Malathi sighed heavily and said.

"What you have said just now made one thing so clear to me! It was just that Neeraja who possessed your Thanuja and made her come into my flat. It was that Neeraja who talked to my son through your Thanuja. I have no doubt in it at all now." With a shocking expression in her face Manorama said.

"I am quite against spirits and paranormal. I just don't know how to take any of this. I still cannot believe that I went to that guy and talked with him." Saritha who was also with Malathi and Sulochana there, said.

"You now a day people cannot believe anything easily." Looking into the face of Sulochana there Manorama said as if she wanted some support to her statement. "There are spirits and there is paranormal in my form opinion."

"Of course, I am also of the same opinion. I have no doubt that our Thanuja was possessed temporarily by that Swaroop's sister, came to your son and talked like that."

"Oh, please don't talk like that! I am feeling very much fear thinking so." With a horrifying expression in her face, Thanuja said.

"I don't want to make you feel terrified but I cannot see any other explanation for your odd behaviour." Manorama said. "My son Aravind and that girl Neeraja were deeply in love. I did not agree to their marriage in the beginning as that Swaroop's family did not appear as a good family to us. But my son Aravind was very much adamant to marry only that girl so I have to agree. A date was also fixed for their marriage also but it has happened like that the girl also died in that accident." she sighed heavily before saying again. "..............my son has become mechanical and he is living life like a robot. He is a chartered accountant, doing a very good job in a big company and handsome also. Many parents are ready to give their daughters to my son but he is not at all ready to marry. He just cannot forget about that Neeraja and thinking about her always."

"It is indeed very much pathetic!" Malathi said with a sorrowful expression in her face. "I got hold of a dairy written by that Swaroop's wife Menaka and we came to know many a thing from it regarding their family." Then she explained to her what all of them have learnt by reading that diary excluding some uncomfortable matters from it.

"Then there is no surprise at all that family left this place on that day so. It is indeed very much pathetic that they met with an accident and died like that." Manorama exclaimed with a sorrowful expression in her face.

"As I said before we did not take the rumour that this flat is haunted seriously, purchased this flat and settled like this. Now it has been confirmed to us not just this flat haunted by the spirits of that Swaroop's family but they possess us also. I just don't know what should we do that the other family members of Swaroop decide to possess the rest of us and there is no guarantee that Thanuja, Prathap and Saritha are not going to be possessed by the same spirits again." Malathi's face was filled with a worrying expression.

"What you have said is true but don't feel unnecessary fear. It is more than one month or so but those spirits did not do any particular harm to you people except some of them possessing some of your family members. You people have got a very beautiful flat at an extremely lower price and don't try to leave it at all." Manorama said.

"That is what exactly we are also thinking!" Malathi said.

There was some silence and none of them preferred to say anything until Manorama talked again.

"My husband used to work as a high school head master in a government school and he died when Aravind was just six years or so aged and he is the only son to us. Then I have been given a teacher job in a government school on compassionate grounds. What all I have got is Aravind and he proved to be very much intelligent and handsome also just like his father. He completed his chartered accountancy with high level marks and could get a very lucrative job in a big company. In fact it was he who purchased this flat taking loan from a bank and I must say financially we are absolutely alright. There are no problems to us." Manorama paused again and everyone there was listening to her eagerly.

"Then he fell in love with that girl Neeraja and I did not feel any surprise. That Neeraja also was a beautiful girl just like your Thanuja. I would not have made any objection to their love and marriage if

I have not come to know anything unpleasant about that Swaroop's family. I heard that Swaroop was not a good guy and he cheated his customers of their money. He wanted to have his own sister in law and was quite against to her marriage with that Saketh. Moreover people used to hear quarrels everyday from his home. So in the beginning I was quite against Aravind's love and his marriage with that girl. But he was quite adamant to marry her and as that girl also did not appear as bad. I thought that it was not better to impose the bad quality of her brother on her and ultimately I agreed to their marriage. Marriage date was also fixed and my son was so happy but suddenly that family died like that! My son has broken, devastated and I already told how he is living. It is one year or so that incident happened but there is no change in him at all." She sighed heavily in the end.

"It is really very much bad! Such an incident should not have taken place in his life." Saritha said.

"He is handsome and intelligent! Everyone can say that by just looking at him. He is a chartered accountant and doing a very good job also. I am thinking to perform his marriage with a nice girl. He is not agreeing to that at all but I am confident that I can make him agree to it." With a meaningful expression in her face Manorama said.

"That is indeed a very nice idea!" Sulochana said and Malathi also nodded her head in agreement.

"Alright. I made you people listen to my pathetic story and spoiled your moods. Now I go." Manorama got off from the chair she sat.

"It is not at all so. We are happy that we have got acquaintance with you." Malathi got off from the chair she sat. "You came first time into my flat. I don't like your going without taking coffee in my home." Then she moved away from that place.

"What you are doing now?" looking into the face of Thanuja who sat opposite to her in the sofa, Manorama asked sipping the coffee given by Malathi.

"I studied degree. I want to do a job but my brother and parents are not agreeing to it." with a smile on her lips Thanuja said.

"A girl of her age should be married, stay in home and be helpful to her family and husband." Sulochana said. "That is what I and my husband also firmly think."

On hearing that Malathi, Thanuja and Manorama also laughed. "That is the way traditional parents always do think and that is the best way of thinking in my opinion." Manorama said.

"Not just her parents my husband and I also are of the same opinion." Malathi said with a smile.

"If majority of the people are thinking like this, what I can do except obliging them?" Saritha said mocking worry and everyone there laughed again.

"If you don't mind, will you please do a favour to me?" looking into the face of Thanuja while sipping the coffee Manorama asked her.

"Don't hesitate ask me aunt." Thanuja said with a small smile on her lips.

"Will you please come to my home sometimes? I have seen some happiness in my son's face while talking with you after a long time. You are almost like that girl and I think he felt as if he was talking with her while he was talking with you."

Instantly Thanuja's face was filled with an uneasy expression. "I try aunty" she said.

"Thank you dear!" Manorama put the finished cup on the table there, said and got off from the chair. "I welcome all your family into my home. Please make time to visit us."

"Sure we do." Malathi said and she also got off from the sofa and Sulochana also stood up.

Then Thanuja, Malathi and Sulochana went with her upto the entrance. After she got into the lift and the doors of the same were closed, they closed the door of the flat, came to their respective places again and sat.

"I have no doubt that very soon she asks our Thanuja to marry her son. Without being told, we can understand that by looking at the expression on her face and the way of her talking." Malathi laughed and said.

"I am also thinking the same. If she has no such idea, she would not have told us about his son's love affair and the failure of it so." Sulochana said.

"Chartered accountancy is a very big qualification aunty. As Aravind is her only son and they have no financial problems also, I can say he would be a good match for our Thanuja" Saritha said.

"Hello, I am not ready to marry a guy who has a love affair already." With an angry expression in her face Thanuja got off from the chair she sat. "I am not planning to go even to his home again. So don't develop such hopes." Then she went away from that place fast.

Chapter-6

Saritha startled when she felt tugged at her legs. When she looked down it was two years or so aged son of Saketh. He hugged her at her legs and looking up at her expectantly.

"I am sorry. I am absolutely sorry." Saketh came there and took his son from her with force before holding him up in his hands. "He was very much attached with that Sirisha. After your dealing with him so on that day in our flat, I am thinking he is mistaking you as her."

"Its alright, no problem at all." Pinching the cheek of Anurag with her right hand, Saritha said and once again Anurag tried to came to her and this time she could not escape from taking him into her hands.

"Oh, please don't vex her." Saketh tried to take his son from her again but he did not obey at all.

"I think you are going into your home now. I come along with you, no problem." Kissing on the right cheek of Anurag, Saritha said.

"I just don't know whether to say sorry or thanks to this." With a troubling expression in his face, Saketh said.

"You need say neither, come." Saritha moved from that place towards the lift there along with Anurag and Saketh just followed her.

"AFTER SIRISHA ENTERED into my life like that, I thought all my problems have been solved. But it has happened so. I can say it has happened just because of that Swaroop. He created problems so to that entire family and they had to leave like that I think. If they did not leave so on that day, Sirisha would not have died along with them."

Anurag fell asleep on the shoulder of Saritha by the time they reached into Saketh's flat and Saketh put him on the bed in the bedroom in a comfortable condition. Then without listening to Saritha he made coffee for both of them in the kitchen and he started talking again while they both were sipping coffee sitting facing each other in chairs in the hall. Even she knew about the story of Saketh and Sirisha, Saritha listened with attention while he was explaining it to her again.

"She told me that his business was in big losses. She often felt fear thinking what was going to happen to her family. Her whole family were quite happy when we both proposed to marry except that bastard!" suddenly there was an angry expression in the face of Saketh.

"I know about this. I know about this through the diary which was written by her sister. We got it in the store room of the house." Saritha said.

"Really! What she has written in that diary?" with gathered frowns and surprise, Saketh asked her and listened eagerly while she was explaining what they came to know in a measured tone.

"My god! This is just confirming my worst fear. The rumours are true! All they are in your flat as spirits! Your coming to me and talking like that on that day also is just proving it." With a horrifying expression in his face Saketh said.

"Mr.Saketh! You are an educated person. Don't give room to such type of beliefs. There are no spirits and there is no paranormal at all." Saritha said with firmness in his voice.

"Then why did you behave so on that day?" Saketh knitted his brows together.

"For the present I cannot give any explanation to that. But just because of that I never believe in spirits." There was the same firmness in her voice.

Immediately there was some disappointing expression in his face, he leaned back in the chair and closed his eyes.

"How much she was aged and how she used to appear?" after few seconds pause, breaking that silence Saritha asked him.

"Twenty two years. Just like your height and width. Her eyes, mouth and nose also just like yours. There is strong resemblance between you both and that might be the reason for Anurag's mistaking you as Sirisha." Saketh said.

"I have no objection to play the role of Sirisha at Anurag occasionally if it makes him feel happy." With a smile on her lips Sirisha said

"I really want you to do like that. It indeed would be a great help" there was sudden grateful expression in the face of Saketh " Anyhow I want to know about you. What you are doing now and why you are in that home?"

"My story is as much pathetic as the story of Sirisha. The only difference is she was divorced and I am a widow. As my step-mother and half brother not allowed me to stay along with them in their house, I am staying with my sister's family like this."

"I am sorry. I am really very much sorry in hearing this." Suddenly Saketh's face was filled with sorrow. "Not just in physique there is similarity in lives also between you and Sirisha. The only other difference is; she has no parents at all."

"My mom died when I was just five years or so aged and my sister was aged eight years or so by then. My dad married again and my step-mother gave birth to a boy after two years or so of the marriage. But from the beginning it was just torture to me and my sister in the hands of my step-mother. My dad has to fight tooth and nail to make us both educated in the way we wanted and he has to fight even more to perform my sister's marriage with my brother in law who is very good guy, well educated and nicely employed. But quite unfortunately one year or so after my sister's marriage my dad expired. After that my step-mother and step-brother's only idea was to get rid of me as fast as possible and they selected a worst fellow for my marriage. As I was also very much eager to escape from them both, I agreed to that marriage but the torture which I have escaped at my step-mother and step-brother was started four fold in my in-law's house. My husband, his parents, his sister all tortured me in the way they wanted. In fact the death of my husband was a relief to me but as I expected my step-mother and half-brother did not agree for my staying with them. After the death of my husband, the torture in my in-law's home has become even more and when my sister invited me into her home I just could not say a no. My sister indeed loves me a lot. But my *bava* (husband of the sister) and his family also are so much good and they just welcomed me into their home. I must say I am feeling very happy in my sister's home." Saritha sighed heavily after explaining all that to him.

"I don't know whether to feel happy or sorrow for your present situation. You have escaped from that torture but how long you can stay in your sister's house in this way?"

"I don't know, I cannot say anything about that." Saritha got off from the chair she sat and said. "Now I have to go. There is a visitor to our home at any time now. I just forgot to tell you two other interesting incidents." Suddenly she remembered about the odd behaviour of Prathap and Thanuja also when she remembered about Sanjana's coming to their home.

"What are they?" Saketh also got off from the chair and asked her looking into her face.

Then she explained in a measured tone the odd behaviour of Prathap at Sanjana and Thanuja at Arvind while Saketh was listening with rapt attention.

"Was it......was it all true?" with an astounding expression in his face Saketh said.

"Of course, Saketh! I read fiction with interest but I have no ability to concoct stories. If you want you may ask my *bava's* brother and sister about it." Saritha smiled. "That girl at whom my *bava's* brother behaved like that wanted to come to our home and see whether she can feel the presence of her lover there. She comes at any moment now."

"It is giving me a new idea! I also come into your home and try to see whether I can feel Sirisha's presence there." Saketh also got off from the chair and said.

"My sincere suggestion to you is please don't develop any belief in spirits and paranormal." With a pleading expression in her face, Saritha said. "Despite myself has an experience like that, I don't believe in spirits. I never believe that either Neeraja or Prathap or I have possessed by devils."

"If it is not so just give me a single reason why you three behaved like that?" Saketh knitted his brows together.

"I already told you that I cannot give you any explanation to that now." Saritha smiled and said. "Anyhow hearty welcome into our house at anytime you want. We are all just so much eager to welcome the residents of this house into our flat."

Then he came along with her upto to the lift, turned back and came into his flat when the lift went down along with her.

"WE HAVE PROPERTIES but our properties in court litigations till six months or so back. We won all the court litigations and all our properties in our hold now. If it were so by the time when Rakesh and his family were suffering so financially, the situation would not have been turned out like that. I sure would have helped them and cleared all their financial problems and at present Rakesh and now would have been quite happy."

After ten minutes or so of Saritha's coming into her flat, Sanjana entered into it along with Prathap. What made them all stunned for a moment was; she was absolutely beautiful! While they were feeling surprise at her beauty like that, she started saying even more surprising things to them consuming the coffee and snacks given by them. Her voice also was as much sweeter as her physique.

"Are you thinking that your parents would have agreed to that if you came forward to help Rakesh's family financially?" Sulochana asked her.

"I am the only daughter to my parents and they have such love and affection on me that they never say 'no' to any of my wishes and desires. My parents have no objection for my marriage with him then also but his brother Swaroop did not agree to it at all as we were paupers at that time."

None of the others there did say anything to her then as they did not know what to say. Sanjana about to say something but then Saritha came there with coffee cups in a tray towards her. Sanjana took a coffee cup from the tray and said thanks.

"I was just irritated and got angry when Prathap came to me and behaved like that. But when he was apologised and explained everything to me, I was just shocked! Still I cannot believe that Rakesh is here as a spirit." Once again there was surprise in the face of Sanjana.

"It is not just he who behaved like that. My sister Thanuja and my *vadina*'s sister Saritha also are possessed by the family members of that Swaroop and behaved like that. I told about that also to you."

"Yes, you did and I remember. That means only one thing! My Rocks is here now." Sanjana got off from the chair and her voice was suddenly with full of emotion. "Where are you Rocks! I just want to see you and talk with you. Please appear to me."

"Relax dear! Relax!" Saritha hurriedly got off form the chair she sat, went near to her and put her right hand around her shoulders. "For the present I cannot give any explanation why Prathap, Thanuja and I behaved like that but just believe me there are no spirits and paranormal at any time. Don't develop any such false beliefs in you."

"You yourself have experienced something like that but you don't believe in it at all!" Sirisha's face was with full of irritation and relieved herself from Saritha's hold around her with force. "Once you cannot give a reasonable explanation for your behaviour so, don't say things like that with me."

"Oh, god! What should I do now?" rubbing the sides of her head with her right hand fingers, Saritha said.

"Shut your bloody mouth and sit straight. She has come here to feel the presence of her late lover and get some peace. You don't try to irritate her by saying things like that." Malathi said angrily.

"But you don't see that she is getting emotional and upset not peace." Saritha also said angrily. "And it is not better to encourage anyone to believe in spirits and paranormal."

"Rakesh, Rakesh, why don't you come and talk with me? I am here for you. Have you forgotten me? Have you lost all your love on me after death? Why don't you appear to me now? I know you are now here." Suddenly Sanjana cupped her face in her hands, broke herself into heavy weeping and slumped herself on the floor there.

Everyone there shocked on her behaviour like that and did not know what to do instantly. But before any of them did anything, Prathap went near to her, sat on his knees beside her before putting his right hand around her shoulders. "If I have forgotten you, why did I contact you through this guy? It is impossible the love in me on you is to lose. Death also cannot make it possible."

It was just like an electric shock to Sanjana, she turned and looked into his face. "Rocks!" she said with a shivering tone.

"Yes, I am. Your Rocks." Prathap smiled and said. "I always want to come to you and contact with you but it is not possible to me to do so without a body and I cannot enter into a body unless it is amicable to me to do that. It is indeed my luck this boy's body is amicable to me to enter to contact with you."

"Rocks......Rocks......you just don't know how much happy I am feeling now." She suddenly hugged him hardly and kissed all over his face vehemently. "I just want you to stay with me all the time like this."

"That is not possible to me. I cannot stay in this body for long. I am a spirit now and I have limitations. You need to understand." Prathap said.

Sanjana's face was filled with deep sorrow and before she said anything, Prathap himself said.

"You have to understand one other thing also." He paused for a second as if to reiterate whatever he was going to say. "I cannot be peaceful if you do worry like this for me all the time. You have to forget me and settle with another guy in your life."

"That is impossible! You too know very well it is impossible." Sanjana said firmly and stood up "How you can say something like that? How you are thinking that I can marry someone else and settle in my life? If it is not for my parents, I would have died the moment you were dead." Her voice was vehement.

"So you want me to suffer like this forever thinking about you. Even you know that you cannot live along with a spirit, why you are adamant like this?" Prathap also stood up to his full height and said looking angrily into the face of Sanjana.

"You tell me one thing, just one thing!" there was the same firmness in her voice then also. "If you were in my place and it was I who died, can you settle with some other girl? Is it is possible to you to do so?"

"I cannot say anything to that now. But.........." he sighed heavily and said. ".........no spirit can take another birth or dissolve itself into universe if it is worrying for something. I do have to worry for you all the time if you remain single worrying about me. If you want my soul to get piece and take another birth or dissolve into universe, you have to marry some other guy , settle in your life and be happy."

"It is not possible to me, it is not possible to me. You are saying something that is impossible to me." This time she only mumbled as she has become completely undecided after hearing from Prathap so.

"But if you love me, you really want me to have peace and relive myself from this spirit body, you must do so. You must marry someone and be happy with him." His voice was with the same firmness.

"Oh, no...........oh,no...........don't say like that!" shaking his shoulders heavily holding with her hands, Sanjana said.

"What's happening? Why we both are holding each other like this?" it was just like Prathap suddenly came to his senses and he instantly relieved from the hold of Sanjana with surprise in his face.

"Her lover once again came into your body bro, she and him have talked many a thing also." Thanuja said coming near to them both.

"I am sorry. I am absolutely sorry." Moving away from him, Sanjana said. "It was I who hold you like that while I have been talking with my Rocks through you."

"Don't worry." Prathap said coming near to her. "Anyhow I am happy that you could meet your lover in this way. Your visit to my house did not go in vain."

"That much is right!" Sanjana was about to say something but then Saritha came there, put her right hand around her shoulders again and said. "First you come and relax yourself for sometime. You have exhausted your energy completely by your heavy emotion till now."

"We all have heard the conversation between you and your lover quite clear dear." Once all they were settled in the sofa and chairs there along with Saritha and Sanjana also, Malathi said. "Your lover's suggestion is absolutely reasonable. You have to forget him, marry someone else and settle in your life."

"You people just don't know how much difficult it is to me to do." Once again there was fully worry expression in the face of Sanjana. "I cannot even imagine forgetting Rakesh and marrying someone else."

"You must remember one thing." Sulochana said. "If you want peace of your lover, you have to do that. As per his saying, he cannot take another birth or dissolve in universe until he stops worrying about you and he just always worries about you if you remain single and worry about him."

Sanjana took her lower lip between her teeth frames and started chewing on it.

"Why do you people suffocate her with your ideas? She needs time to take such decisions and it takes time to find a suitable guy also. For the present, just leave her to her own thinking and god certainly shows a way." Prathap said.

"Indeed a very nice suggestion!" with an appreciative expression in her face, Saritha said.

"Now I go." Sanjana got off from the chair she sat. "And thank you all very much for letting me to come to your home and talk with my Rocks like that."

"You are always welcome to come into our home whenever you want............" Malathi also got off from the chair she sat. "............even we cannot say that you can talk with your Rocks every time like this."

"Once again thank you all. Now I have to go." After saying that Sanjana walked away from that place and Prathap also went along with her.

"PLEASE COME INSIDE my dear. Why do you stand there?" Manorama got off from the chair she sat, came near to her and said when Thanuja was at the threshold of their house. Just like on the previous occasions Thanuja came to their home on that Sunday while Manorama and Aravind were talking in the hall and the front doors of the flat were opened wide.

Thanuja came fast, slumped herself in the chair in which Manorama sat till then before putting her both hands around Aravind's neck and kissed on his right cheek. Aravind shocked and looked into her face.

"How long you do worry about me like this Aravind? Cannot you understand how do I feel if you remain worrying about me always?" Looking into his face straight Thanuja asked him.

"How can....how can .....I remain without worrying and thinking about you? If it were you in my place can you do that?" Arvaind asked her as he understood with whom he was talking then without being told.

Manorama also understood that and observing them both with interest standing a little away.

"If I were you in your place, I sure do marry again and settle in my life even however difficult it is to me to do so. I know doing like that is very much impossible to me and painful but I sure do like that if it gives peace to you." With firmness Thanuja said. "Then cannot you marry someone and settle with her if that gives me peace? I just feel worry and sorry all the time as long as you remain single and worry about me. You must marry someone, settle in your life atleast for me." Suddenly there was pleading expression in the face of Thanuja

Aravind leaned back, closed his eyes with deep frowns on his forehead.

"You said.....you said a very nice thing!" Manorama came near to them and said. "It is not just you I am also suffering a lot seeing him like this." Then she put her both hands on the shoulders of Thanuja and squeezed them tightly. "Ask him to come out of his worry. Make him understand how much I am also suffering seeing him suffer like that."

As if that action of Manorama galvanised something in her, Thanuja turned her head, freed the chair and stood up with a surprising expression in her face.

"Once again I am in your home! Why it is happening to me time and again like this?" the surprise was just so in the face of Thanuja.

"Nothing happened to you." Manorama said. "As that Neeraja cannot see my son worrying like this, she got into your body again, came here and talked with him."

"My mom is right." Aravind opened his eyes, got off from the chair and said. "I have talked with my Neeraja all this time through you."

"My god! What is this?" Thanuja took her head into both of her hands, swayed on her left side and unless Manorama took her into her both hands she would have fallen on the floor there. Manorama made her sit in the chair there in which she sat before.

"Relax, relax my dear! There is no necessity to you to feel like this." Manorama put her right hand on the shoulder of Thanuja.

"Why, why that Neeraja every now and then does prefer to come into me and make you people disturbed?" with gathered frowns Thanuja looked into the faces of Aravind and Manorama.

"You did not disturb me I must say." With firmness Aravind said. "In fact I came out of my distress a lot by talking with my Neeraja in such a way through you. I really felt happy."

"Okay then." Thanuja freed the chair and stood up. "I go to my home now."

"Just wait. I want you to take some coffee in my home and then go. I don't know what's the reason but you are appearing so weak." Once again making her sit in that chair Manorama said.

"No aunty. I am not feeling weak. I can go into my home." Thanuja said but without listening to her Manorama went away from there.

"Thank you, thank you very much!" sitting in the chair beside Thanuja, Aravind said.

"For what?" Thanuja knitted her brows looking into his face.

"You gave me the pleasure to talk with my Neeraja through you." There was sudden happy expression in the face of Aravind. "I am not feeling much bad as I can talk with my Neeraja like this."

"Do you hundred percent believe that it is your Neeraja who talked to you through me?"

"Why do you doubt that?" frowns gathered on the forehead of Aravind.

"My psychologist aunt Saritha is not feeling like that. She is saying it is a sort of psychological disorder."

"Despite being possessed by a family member of that Swaroop's family, she is talking like that." Manorama who came there with a coffee cup in a saucer then said while handing it over to Thanuja.

"Yes, mom. I remember. You said that to me. Not just this girl, her brother and her aunt also possessed by the family members of that Swaroop. What more proof we need to say that it is no one else but my Neeraja?" once again Aravind's face was with full of happiness.

"I am feeling happy that you can get peace by talking with your Neeraja in this way." Making the small sips of the coffee, Thanuja said. "But it is quite embarrassing to me. What the people around think if I come into your home like this and talk with your son in this way?"

"You are absolutely right." Looking straight into the face of Thanuja, Manorama said. "There is only one solution to this problem."

"What is that aunty?" by then Thanuja finished the coffee, put the empty cup beside the chair, stood up and looked into the face of Manorama.

"Marry my son." Manorama said straightly. "Then no one would say anything."

"Aunty what you are talking?" with a startling expression in her face Thanuja said.

"Mom, this is not the way to talk with that girl." Aravind angrily said.

"I said what I am feeling in my heart as I cannot keep my feelings in me for long." Without any change in her expression or face, Manorama said. "You clearly heard what that Neeraja wants. She can get peace only after you marry and settle in your life and I cannot see anyone else fit to fill that Sirisha's place except this girl."

"Bye aunty. I meet you people again." After saying that without looking back Thanuja came out of that place.

"You are right mom." After few seconds of Thanuja going away from that place, Aravind opened his mouth. "I really do feel happy as I can interact with my Neeraja through this girl. But why does she interest in me? I am deeply in love with someone else and cannot forget her. My main reason to marry this girl also is to talk and spend time with Neeraja but not with love on her."

"But remember one thing Aravind your Neeraja cannot be peaceful until you marry someone and stop worrying about her." Manorama said "You must marry someone and settle in your life again. Even not for me, you have to do that atleast for the Sirisha's peace and relieve her from that spirit body." After saying that she went away from that place and Aravind wearily slumped in his chair, leaning back and closed his eyes.

Chapter-7

"**I** want you people do a favour to me."

In that night time while all of them were talking in the hall there, Saritha suddenly said that and they looked at her then. Saritha's face was with frowns and an odd expression.

"What favour you want from us?" looking into her face Anand asked her with a smile on his lips. "Just feel free to press that. But we reserve our promise until we hear it."

"Will you people please make your Saritha agree to marry my Saketh and make him come out of his misery and problems? Saketh is a very good man and your Saritha can be so happy with him."

There came startled expressions into the faces of the people there.

"What it is that we have to make our Saritha agree to marry your Saketh? You are Saritha yourself." So far Malathi understood what happened along with all the others there but asked so as if for confirmation.

"Now I am not Saritha. I am Saketh's lover Sirisha in your Saritha's body." With the same modulation in her voice Saritha said. "My Saketh is very much worrying and distressing himself with my thoughts. I cannot be peaceful at all if he is like that. My soul can get peace only after he settles in his life happily again with someone. And I am convinced that your Saritha is that someone."

"But I don't know whether Saritha agrees to it or not." Malathi said with gathered frowns. "Of course, she also needs someone to lead her life but I cannot say anything until I talk with her."

"We don't know much about that Saketh. Unless we know about him in full, we cannot make a promise like that to you." Sulochana said.

"Saketh is a very good guy. You people need no doubt in that at all. Your Saritha will be so happy in her life and Saketh hundred percent deserves her." Saritha said.

"You don't worry. I look into this matter." Anand said. "I go to that Saketh and talk with him. If I feel it is okay, I promise you that I make them both man and wife."

"Thank you, thank you very much!" suddenly there was a happy expression in the face of Saritha but in seconds it disappeared and she fell on her left side on the shoulder of Malathi with closed eyes.

"I think Sirisha's soul left my sister's body." Malathi said while tapping gently on the left cheek of Saritha.

"What, what happened sister?" once again Saritha made herself straight on the sofa and looked into her sister's face with confusion.

"Once again you have been exposed to your psychological disorder. You talked just like that Sirisha again." With a smile on her face Malathi said.

"But we are not going to take it as your psychological disorder. We are taking it as Sirisha talked through you and I am going to fulfil the promise I made to her." Anand said.

"What promise you made to her?" frowns gathered on the forehead of Saritha.

Then it was Malathi who explained everything to her including Sirisha's wish and Anand's promise to her.

"You just have to listen to us." Saritha was about to say something but before that Sulochana said. "Anand would talk with that guy and make some inquires also. If we all think that he is a nice guy, you must agree to your marriage with him."

"Why I deny it, why I deny that at all? If he agrees to marry me, I feel myself so lucky." Saritha hung her head and said "But still I feel it is a sort of psychological disorder in me but not that Sirisha."

"WE ARE ALL SO HAPPY now that Saketh agreed to marry you and you are going to be settled in your life. I want to go to temple, then to some shopping and then to a movie. I want you, Thanuja, uncle and aunty also come along with me." Looking into the face of Saritha, Malathi said.

Anand went to Saketh, talked with him and inquired about him before telling him what Sirisha expressed to them through Thanuja. Once he knew that it was the wish of Sirisha herself, Saketh did not object more. What all need to be done now was fix an auspicious time to make them both man and wife.

"I have no objection to that. It is indeed time for some celebration." Sulochana said.

"As a temple also is included in the program, I am interested. I come." Sudarshan said.

"I am also in." Thanuja said.

"But sister, please excuse me for this time. I have headache and want to take rest in home. Next time we go." With an uneasy expression in her face Saritha said.

In fact she phoned to Saketh and asked him to come home early on that day to spend some time together and he agreed to come home by twelve o clock or so. So she wanted to stay at home itself.

Malathi guessed something like that and refrained the smile that was forcing onto her lips with force. "As you wish it then." She said.

"Why don't you plan this on some holiday *Vadina*? Brother and I also can come with you." Prathap imitated an irritating expression on his face.

"Next time sure but sorry for this time." Malathi said.

When all of them were left the flat on their programs, Saritha left all alone in the flat. She went into her room, fell flat on the bed while resting her right hand's arm on her forehead.

For the first time, after a long time, she was once again very much happy. In all respects Saketh was quite different with her late husband. He was tall and handsome, educated, suitably employed, having properties and in addition to all this kind hearted. She has to consider herself so lucky that she could marry a person like him. His having love on that Sirisha did not make her worry much as she was confident that she could make him forget about her and think about her only.

One thing she was thinking about then was, in fact quite predominant in her thoughts all the time was sex! Except knowing about it and thinking about that, she has no experience in sex before her marriage. But those thoughts and knowledge itself used to create so much of excitement and thrill in her. Most of her friends have sexual experience in that and some of them have abortions also and while they were explaining that, the excitement and thrill in her used to become more and she also so much wanted to have it. If she could manage to get a guy to satisfy her urge in those days, she would not have taken a back step at all. But before marriage there was no chance at all to her to have it from a guy.

She could not think much of sexual joy when her marriage was settled with Nandagiri considering his lean and short personality. She learnt from her friends that main thing would be matching with a person's personality and a big man does have a big thing and a small man does have a small thing. Without being told by anyone Saritha knew very well that a big thing explores the depth well and give more joy than a small thing. But she was very much desperate to escape from the torture in the hands of her step-mother and half-brother so agreed to the marriage with that Nandagiri. If nothing else she has expected atleast a kind heart and good treatment in his hands.

When it was come to sex, it was more disappointing and sordid with him than she expected. What new information she has got on after the marriage was, he was a heavy drunkard and his concentration was only on drinking all the time but nothing else. On the first night, he said he entered into her but she did not feel anything! On the very few occasions afterwards, when they both tried it together, every time he said he entered into her but she knew he did not. When she said he did not and he was just imagining that, he used to get lot of anger on her and beat her. He never let her to take the initiative to make his rod properly enter into her main thing so there was never a chance to her to know whether it was actually happening to her or not. Once sex became a nightmare to her in his hands, she has forgotten about that leaving him absolutely to his drinking and thinking.

It was as much horrible as sex in other matters of her life also while living with him. The four of them comprising her husband, his mother, his father and sister used to torture her making her maximum distressed as that gave them particular sadistic pleasure. The only one person on the earth at that time to tell about her distress was her sister Malathi only and many a time Malathi demanded her to leave that house and come to her home but Saritha did not want to trouble her sister and suffered like that as long as her husband was alive. It was indeed a big relief when he died with the disease he got developed with his heavy drinking with all sorts of wine. But the torture in the hands of her in laws' reached its motto and she could not bear that anymore. She knew there was no chance to go to her step-mother's house but when her sister Malarthi once again demanded to come to her home and stay with her, she could not deny.

Even while she was suffering a lot in the hands of her husband and in her in laws' hands and after the death of her husband also, her body used to burn with the desire to have full-fledged sex with someone. Her husband was an utter failure in satisfying her in sex but he was successful in one thing! He made the urge in her raised even more and sometimes she was so much desperate to have it with someone and if she has got someone, she sure would have got her urge satisfied with him even she knew it was quite unethical and immoral!

Now also she was feeling just like that. She was feeling happy as Saketh was a tall, stout and handsome guy and by the size of his physique she could assume how much his thing would be. On some occasions she saw the thing of Nandagiri, it was so small matching with his body size and as he said even he entered into her, there was no surprise she did not feel it at all between the lips of her main-thing as it was that much small. It surely would not be like that with Saketh! His thing sure would be big and she could feel its sweeping up and down between the lips of her main-thing hundred percent! And Saketh may allow her to play an active part during sex and that was what she indeed wanted.

Then she suddenly remembered one thing that one of her friends said and it made her feel even more happy. Sex in the hands of an experienced guy would be more pleasurable than with an inexperienced guy. She compared her experience with the son of her neighbour and the husband of her sister and came to the opinion. It was the first time to the son of her neighbour and he burst even before putting his thing at the entrance of her main thing. He could not manage it in hers more than few seconds when at last he put it through.

But it was not so with the husband of her sister, her *bava* who caused two children to her sister in three years span possibly fucking her more than hundred times in the meanwhile. Her friend's expectation did not go wrong when she had it with her bava and she just did not know how long he moved his bulged thing between her tightly closed vaginal lips but all the time it was just pleasure, pleasure and pleasure to her! Not just that, her friend said, it was just so to her that he knew about her body more than herself might be just because of his acquaintance with her sister's naked body in a full-fledged way.

Having a son now undoubtedly meant that Saketh has good experience in sex with his wife as it was rare that woman would get pregnancy at the first time fucking itself. Moreover, that Sirisha and himself also would have sex in between themselves and she could guess that much. For the present she was quite optimistic to have best sex experience in the hands of Saketh.

There was fire all over her body then and she was waiting for the phone call from Saketh. She asked him to come straight home from the bank without taking Anurag from that baby care and he would have guessed for what she was asking him to come like that. He said that he would phone to her as soon as he came into his flat and he promised to come by twelve itself. She took her cell phone which was laid beside her and lit its screen. It was only ten thirty and she felt so much impatient. She just did not know how to cope with this burning desire until he came. She sighed heavily, turned face down and pressed her left cheek to the pillow while pressing her chest part to the bed there heavily while widening her thighs to the maximum. Then disturbing her absolutely, the sound of calling bell reached her ears.

Saritha could not guess who has come! None of the family members would return this fast to home. Saketh said he would phone to her as soon as he came and he asked her to come into his flat then not he into her flat. Even he preferred to come into her flat, it was too early to him to come as his promised arrival time was twelve. Sighing heavily Saritha got off from the bed, went near to the doors and opened them wide.

"Oh, *bava*! You!" Saritha's face was filled with surprise! "I am not expecting you now. You are supposed to come in the evening."

"You may not expect this" once he came inside Anand closed the doors, latched them and put the bolt. "But life is just that having unexpected things now and then."

"You are right *bava*" Saritha laughed and walked inside of the house. "Anyhow what happened? Suddenly your office declared holiday on this day?"

"No, of course." Anand said. "I took leave myself and came home."

"What *bava*? What happened?" Saritha came near to him anxiously. "Are not you feeling alright? Are you feeling some headache or fever?" she put her right palm on his forehead and asked.

"Yes, I am not feeling alright. I cannot feel alright until I complete what I could not finish on that day." Suddenly Anand took her into his hug and kissed on her lips straight.

"What *bava*? What bloody hell is this?" Saritha tried to relieve herself from his hug but it was so strong around her and however much she tried, Anand's grip around her was becoming that strong.

"Just listen to me. It is going to be wonderful for you. I can give it to you in the best way than anyone else. That Saketh also cannot do it better than I. It will be so good in my hands to you and just be obeyed. I am not going to leave you without having it and it is the best time to both of us to have it together."

He tightened his both hands to his might, now his left hand palm was between her both buttocks and he was massaging the gap between them. However much she was against to have it with him, his touch like that and especially his rubbing on the huge canal between her buttocks was making pleasure waves sweep all over her body.

"Don't think that you can escape from me just like the last time. This time I am not going to leave you until I satisfy my desire in all respects." Making her move towards his bedroom using all his force Anand said.

"What the bloody hell you are talking? You never did a nasty thing like this on me and my *bava* never even think to this type of thing!" Saritha managed to say even all the while trying to escape from his grip but Anand was successful to make her laid on the bed and put himself on the top of her.

"You know about your bava very well, don't you, you fucking liar?" even he was struggling a lot to keep her under his weight, Anand managed to kiss on her lips again. It was not just his brute strength that made her subdued like that to him then. The burning desire in her still then was also making her body amicable to him. Against her will and wish her body wanted that pleasure then and there, irrespective of the point who was giving it.

"I never liked your marriage with that Saketh. But you people forced me to agree for your marriage with him. Before he fucks, let me have the pleasure of fucking your cunt atleast for once. I never do ask for it again." Still using his full force and pinning her down under his weight, Anand said.

"You bastard, scoundrel......now I understood! You are not my *bava*! You are Swaroop in the body of my *bava*." Saritha yelled and tried to throw him away from her body once again in vain. "But I am not that girl Sirisha. I am a different person."

"But that Sirisha is identifying herself in you and you are also just like her. She is dead now and there is no chance to me to have her at present. I can have the same pleasure by having you also." He managed to take her petticoat up until her hips and she was absolutely naked in her under-parts then as she did not wear a drawer. But he has to stand on his knees to unzip and unbutton his pants for the necessary activity and for a moment he has forgotten about the consequences and stood on his knees between her thighs, unhooked and unzipped his pants and made it down. What all he needed to do then was to make his drawer also down and put himself onto her again.

But she was waiting herself all the time for a moment like that and did not waste it. Once she has become free of his weight like that and her both legs were also free of her petticoat and saree, she kicked him with her right leg in the middle part of him with all her strength. He fell back on the floor with a thump, hitting his head strongly on the floor there and in the immediate instant Saritha ran into the kitchen, went to the shelf there and took a knife from it and positioned it in her hands so to pierce her *bava* with it if he would come and tried anything on her then. She was feeling fear also as she has seen his falling down on the floor and hitting his head there with a sound and she could guess it was a big hig. Anything could happen with such a hit of the head to the floor there. She just did not know whether to feel fear or relief when her *bava* entered into the kitchen with his clothes adjusted and a distressing expression on his face.

"I can say what happened." Looking into her face, Anand said with a weakened voice. "Swaroop entered into my body and tried a rape attempt on you. Then you..........."

"Sorry *bava*. I have to kick you like that." Saritha said still holding the knife like that. "I felt fear that some heavy damage happened to you. I heard the sound of your head hitting the floor there."

"I think there is not much damage even I am feeling terrible pain here." Rubbing the right side of his head with his right hand Anand said. "Anyhow you did a nice thing! That Swaroop is a worst guy and he would have finished what he started if you did not kick me like that then."

"I am still very much sorry *bava*. Even however much necessary it was, I should not have kicked you like that. Are you sure there is no damage to your head now?" Saritha knitted her brows together and there was a sorrowful expression in her face but she did not leave the knife at all.

"You never mind about that. If necessary I get my head examined by a doctor." He laughed and she knew it was forced. "Anyhow you need not feel fear anymore. That Swaroop left my body and I am your *bava* now."

"No *bava*. That Swaroop may once again come into your body who knows? I am not going to leave this knife and move away from here until all the other people come here." At that moment she has completely forgotten about her arrangement with Saketh.

Both of them did not know how much of time passed, indulging themselves in all types of thoughts but suddenly startled when they heard calling bell sound. Anand got off from the chair he sat and went away from that place.

"It is Saketh." After few seconds Anand came into the kitchen again and said looking into the face of Saritha. "He said that you asked him to come early on this day so he came. He phoned to you many a time but as that call is not attended, he came straight here."

"Yes, he is right." Saritha put the knife in the shelf there and said. "As I have left my cell phone in the other room I could not attend it."

"You may better come and meet him. He is feeling little worried as you did not attend his phone calls." With concern in his face Anand said.

Saritha just could not remain without putting her hands around Saketh's neck and kissing on his right cheek as soon as she saw him. Even he felt surprise and embarrassed, Saketh also put his hands around her and took her near to him. They both did not bother much about Anand's presence there.

"*Bava* would you mind if I go with Saketh and spend sometime with him?" still holding Saketh like that, Saritha asked Anand looking into his face. It was surprising to her that she was not at all feeling odd to hold Saketh like that before her *bava*.

"I don't mind even you spend your whole day with him." Anand laughed and said. "You both are going to become wife and husband, who would object to it?"

IN THE BEGINNING SHE was not but later Saritha could not remain telling about her *bava*'s rape attempt on her. "That Swaroop in my *bava* almost succeeded in that! If I have not kicked him like that, he would have succeeded in it hundred percent." In the end after she explained about the rape attempt on her, she said.

"He is the only bad guy in his home and I don't feel surprise in his attempting that thing on you." Saketh's face was filled with anger. "He tried to rape Sirisha on one occasion and she could escape then. He tried tooth and nail to prevent her marriage with me to have her himself but all his family members forced him to agree with it. You are almost just like her in his house and he tried to have you through your *bava*. Luckily you escaped from that rape attempt."

Once again the burning desire in her was at its motto and she was so much desperate to feel his thing in her. She wanted to know it would not be a failure or disappointment in his hands as it was in the hands of her late husband Nandagiri.

"Thank you very much to come like this at my request." Thinking furiously how to instigate him for that, Saritha said.

"We both are going to be man and wife. We need not thank each other for anything." He smiled.

"Its alright then." She smiled and nodded her head but immediately a serious expression took place in her face. "Are you really interested in marrying me? Is it is not a marriage just because of that Sirisha's request."

"It is not so." Saketh nodded his head in negation. "Even Sirisha did not request like that I want to marry you if you agree. Anurag need a mother and I am ready to do anything for his happiness."

"So it is a marriage for your son but not for you and me." Saritha said with firmness. "If it is so, I don't think we can be happy like a man and wife."

"No, it is not so." Saketh hurriedly said. "The main reason for my marrying you is Anurag, I agree. But don't think we cannot live happily together as man and wife. I am confident that we both can be happy together as man and wife."

"Can you prove it now? Can you prove it now to me that you can treat me as your wife also not just as mother to Anurag. If you can prove it like that, I feel so happy to become your wife and live along with you. Otherwise, I have to rethink my decision."

"Just tell me how can I prove it to you? If there is a way to prove it to you, I hundred percent do that." Saketh hastily said and the sudden anxiousness in his face made her understand how much he intended to marry her.

Saritha's heart beat increased and her whole body was with a sort of thrill. She just framed the sentences to ask him to let him know about her desire.

"Can you do sex to me in a full-fledged manner now itself without thinking about that Sirisha? If you can do it, I believe that you can treat me as your wife always forgetting about that Sirisha hundred percent."

"It is impossible to me to forget about Sirisha and she always stays in my heart." Suddenly there was firmness in his voice. "But despite that, I can treat you as my wife hundred percent and can do sex to you also hundred percent. If that is what I need to do to you to convince you that I can be your committed and loving husband, I have no objection to that."

"Alright then." It was just like some magic power in her making her move, she got off from the chair she sat, went near to him and put her hands around his neck and kissed on his right cheek after slumping herself on the sofa beside him. "I want it to be proved as fast as possible."

After that while he was leading her from that place into his bedroom and laying her on the bed, she was just like a doll in him. She did not object while he was taking the last garment also from her body but when she became absolutely nude, she felt so much of shame and closed her face with her hands. But as there was no action from him after that, she removed her hands from her face and looked at him and he stood beside the bed and was removing his clothes one after one from his body and at that moment there was only cut-drawer on his body. Her mouth was dried and she has to wet her lips with the tip of her tongue while she was looking at the outline of his bulged penis under the fabric of her cut-drawer. Without bothering about anything, he removed his cut-drawer upto his knees first and then from his whole body. When he stood up to his full height, her mouth dropped open looking at his bulged penis! It was very much big and bulged matching with his body size and she felt fear for a moment whether her poor thing could accommodate that.

"My late wife not but Sirisha and I loved to have sex absolutely naked." Coming near to her he said.

"But your rod is that much big and I am feeling fear that my poor little thing cannot accommodate that!" even she was feeling so much urge to have it as fast as possible but the apprehension in her was genuine then.

"My late wife and Sirisha also felt fear like that at the first time but I proved it wrong to both of them. I am going to prove it like that to you also." He laughed and said.

Then he proved it! When he managed his bulged thing deep into her vagina, she understood he was right. But it did not happen immediately. After enjoying each and every part of her youthful body in a methodical way, after making her feel fear that she might die with pleasure, he put himself in that main job. That Nandagiri did not do even hundred percent of what Saketh did! He proved every word of what her friend said that it would be just wonderful in the hands of an experienced man. This guy has experience with two women so far so she did not feel surprise at his experience in that but his having experience in that with two women before was creating an odd feeling in her.

She could not remain without letting out pleasure groans while his bulged thing was making fierce up and down movements in her tightly closed vaginal lips. She did not how much time of has passed but it was only abundant pleasure to her all the time. The movements from his side were that fierce and forcible and sometimes she felt fear that her under-parts may rip opened!

Suddenly there were two or three even more fierce movements hitting her hard at her down parts and she felt tremendous shivering of his thing inside of her. Even she did not feel like that with Nandagiri at any moment, she understood he got his release! Immediately he sighed heavily and became like an emptied sack on the top of her.

"Thank you very much!" holding him gently with both of her hands and kissing on his right cheek smoothly she said. "You proved yourself hundred percent! I have no doubt now that we both can live so happily as wife and husband."

"I proved another thing also to you, did not I?" he tried to slid on the left side of her as his thing completely came out of her socket by then but she restrained him by tightening her grip around him. His late wife and Sirisha also wanted him to stay like that for some time even after that thing was over, he understood that and remained so. "I proved that your poor little thing can accommodate my big bulged thing completely, did not I?"

"Of course, you proved that also." She once again kissed on the same cheek and said.

"But dear, one thing!" this time she did not restrain him when he tried to slid and he still hugged her closely from her left side. "You were just tight as if you have no experience ever in it."

"I really doubt whether my late husband ever managed to put that in it." she turned towards him and explained him about her experience with Nandagiri. "He always said he did that but I never felt anything in me. He never let me do anything and see what was happening so I did not know whether it took place or not. What my strong belief is; he never fucked me."

"If your strong belief is true......" he hugged her strongly and kissed on her right cheek. "............I just fucked a hundred percent virgin."

IN THE NIGHT OF THAT day, when they were all together at the dining table, it was Anand who explained to them all what he tried on Saritha.

"I know that Swaroop is a bad guy. But I did not expect at all that he would venture such type of a thing by possessing you!" with a horrifying expression in her face, looking into the face of Anand, Malathi said.

In fact, all the other people also were with such horrifying expressions in their faces.

"At his first attempt on that Sirisha he failed and we don't know how she escaped at that time. Now he failed in his attempt by possessing me. I am thinking that he is considering our Saritha as that Sirisha and I apprehend that he doesn't stop looking for an opportunity to have her again."

"You are absolutely right!" the fearful expression in the face of Malathi was intensified even more. "What is the solution to this problem?"

"Don't leave Saritha all alone in the home until she marries Saketh and settle with him." Anand said.

"You are right of course." Malathi nodded her head. "That solves the problem."

"But if he is fixed to have me that much feeling me as his Sirisha......." Saritha said with a fearful expression in her face. ".........I don't think that he leaves me even after my marriage."

"This is also something worth considering." Malathi said. "I try to find a solution to this problem forever and you don't worry."

Chapter-8

"I must say it is because of my Rocks wish but I hundred percent try to be your faithful wife and lover. Just think about how it is that we both become man and wife?" on that day Sanjana asked Prathap while they both were taking coffee in the same canteen, at the same table in the same condition. In those few days they both became good friends also.

Prathap did not say anything but remained silent sipping his coffee.

"I know it is odd to you to marry a girl who is so much in love with a guy. But that guy is now no more and his spirit can be peaceful only after I settle in my life married. I am thinking to fulfil his wish, though it is very much difficult to me to do like that, I want to do for the happiness of my Rocks. I can feel somehow happy and relaxed if I marry you as I can talk with my Rocks also through you sometimes."

"After he expressed his wish like that through me to you in my house on that day, Rocks did not come into my body again. He may never come again into my body." Prathap said amidst his sips.

"Still I prefer to marry only you if I ever marry for the happiness of my Rocks." With gathered frowns Sanjana said. "Rocks saw something of him in you so he came into your body. So I feel happy to marry you than anyone else to make my Rocks happy."

"Your Rocks is full of your heart." By then Prathap finished his coffee and put the empty cup on the table in between. "So I don't think that you can love me with full of your heart feeling about Rocks like that."

"Of course agree, my heart is full of my Rocks and Rocks will be in me like that forever." With firmness Sanjana said. "But he feels happy only if live with my partner happy. I want to keep my Rocks happy, relieve him from his spirit body so I am sure be happy with you giving place to you also in my heart. So hundred percent I love you and be happy with you. Please agree to this." With sudden pleading expression in her face in the end, Sanjana said.

"I agree, alright." With a smile on his lips Prathap said. "Once having that Prathap like that in me, I am also feeling an unknown bond with him and I also want to make him feel happy."

Then Sanjana got off from the chair she sat, came near to him, put her hands around his neck and kissed on his head.

"If you want to show your love on me, there are better place than this to do that." Prathap relieved her hold around him and got off from the chair she sat. "Just see how the people around here are looking at us now?"

There were only few people in that canteen then but they were looking at them both with sort of interest seeing what Sanjana did to him just then. Noticing that, Sanjana's cheeks were blushed deeply.

"Come, we go away from here now." Pulling him from there holding his right hand with her right hand, Sanjana said.

Then Prathap followed her silently from that place.

"YOU ARE GOING TO HAVE it from me just like from the last one week or so. I don't allow you to go to that dirty woman again."

While Sudarshan was trying to go away from that room, Sulochana blocked his way holding his right hand with both of her hands said.

"It is not so with you as it is with that woman to me. Moreover you are having problems also. Why don't you let me have it from her as it keeps you also peaceful?" Sudarshan knitted his brows together.

"My husband having illicit sexual affairs with another woman never keeps me peaceful. Of course I have problems but I suffer the pain to keep you refrain from committing that sin again and again with that bitch. Come, have it with me." Pulling him towards the bed, Sulochana said angrily.

"Like son like father. That dirty Swaroop did not take a back step to have his wife's sister. You go even to a watch man's wife to satisfy your urge." She said while he was positioning himself on the top of her.

"Why do you talk like that even while accommodating me also?" he said angrily and put himself into action.

When it was finished, he got off from her bed, went near to his bed and put himself on that and in the immediate instant he was snoring. After observing him few seconds like that she also fell asleep.

"IT SEEMS FOR THE LAST few days you are out of sorts, what happened aunty?" looking into the face of Sulochana, Malathi asked her while they both were in kitchen sipping coffee. By that time Sudarshan was in his room, Thanuja and Saritha went out on some marketing work, Prathap went to college and Anand to his office.

Sulochana's face was blushed and filled with deep uneasy expression but she did not prefer to talk anything.

"I can understand that there is something aunty, why don't you tell me about it?" Malathi knitted her brows, put the coffee cup on the dining table and balanced her both arms on the table in between.

"I just don't know how to tell this. I still cannot believe whether it has been really happening or just my dream." Sulochana also put her unfinished coffee cup on the table, leaned back in the chair and sighed heavily.

"First let me know about it. Then I try to tell you whether it is reality or just your dream."

"For the last one week or so everyday I have a dream like thing that I have been having it with your uncle. But it was just so real and not like a dream at all. My real feeling at that time was someone else was in me during that time and having that with your uncle." Sulochana gave a pause and her face blushed even more with shame.

Malathi did not say anything but she could understand what Sulochana meant.

"I want to think that it is absolutely my dream but there was some physical disturbance there. In fact......." she paused for a second once again as it was very much difficult to say to her. ".......there were traces of semen also."

"Okay then. What's more?"

"I asked your uncle whether he has been having it with me during the night. He said that he also has been having dream like sexual experience and wanted to take it just as his dream. But he also could see physical disturbance at that place making him understand that he really has been having it with me."

"That means......" Malathi laughed and said. ".........you both are having it together but in a dream like state. Anyhow what's wrong? You both are man and wife and no one can say its wrong even at whatever age you both may be."

"I am feeling fear for two things here Malathi." once again Sulochana's face was with full of apprehension. "I heard about the story of that Swaroop's parents. I have no doubt that it were his parents who have been having sex like that through me and your uncle. The very idea that we have been possessed by devils and are acting according their wishes itself is creating very much fear in me. Next thing.........." she paused for a second before saying again. "...........what happens if I become pregnant at this age?"

"I don't think that you do become pregnant at this age aunty." Malathi also was feeling uneasily after hearing her so.

"Don't say like that. There are women who have become pregnant at their seventies also. I feel very much awkward if I become pregnant now."

"For your second fear, we do go and consult a gynaecologist aunty. We do as per the directions of that gynaecologist. I hope that you did not become a pregnant yet and even you were, the gynaecologist gives a suggestion to us. She sure does suggest some post contraceptive to you if you both have participated in sex without your knowledge in your future." Malathi paused for a second "For your first fear, I have to think about that aunty. I think about that and try to find out a solution to that also."

"Please do that Malathi. Please try to find a solution to this spirits problem in our house. Even more danger is with that Swaroop. I am also apprehending just like Saritha. He may not leave her even after her marriage with Saketh also."

"You are absolutely right aunty." Malathi got off from the chair she sat. "Let me think over it for sometime. I hope that I sure find a solution to this problem." And by then itself an idea was formed in the mind of Malathi.

"I JUST DON'T KNOW WHAT'S the problem to you to agree your marriage with that guy!" Anand angrily said. "He is a chartered accountant working in a big company. No doubt he is handsome also. His mother and himself both are willing to make you his wife."

Manorama met Anand and Malathi when they were at home and requested them to make Thanuja agree to marry Aravind. She said to them that Aravind also agreed to marry Thanuja as that was the strong wish of Neeraja.

"But we all know that Neeraja is full in his heart. How can I marry someone even after knowing his heart is with full of some other girl?

He wants to marry me only because that Neeraja asked him to marry again." Thanuja also has become angry.

"I agree that there is a point in your saying." Malathi said. "But that Neeraja is not alive now and her strongest wish is that he should marry and live his life happily with that girl. So he sure looks after you well Thanu which you need to understand."

"I need not understand but I need to compromise myself to marry that guy." The angry expression was just so in the face of Thanuja. "You cannot get a guy like him unless you give huge dowry and his mother wants his happiness so I need to be compromised myself to marry that Aravind."

"You are not going to get any loss by being compromised sis." Prathap said. "I talked with him and I understood. You can be hundred percent happy with that Aravind."

"I cannot think as you are thinking Prathap. I cannot live with a guy whose heart is full with another girl."

"It is a difficult thing to you Thanuja, I agree." Saritha said. "But giving happiness to other people is a great thing indeed. If you can marry that Aravind, you can make lot many people happy including the spirit of that Neeraja if you assume really there is the spirit of her. As you are not in love with anyone yet just see whether you can compromise yourself to marry that Aravind."

Thanuja took her lower lip between her teeth frames and frowns were gathered on her forehead. After few seconds she released her lip and said "I want to talk with Aravind. Once I have full-fledged talking with that Aravind, I let you guys know about my decision."

"IT IS NOT SO I DON'T like you Aravind. I have no objection to marry you if your heart is not full of that Neeraja. Moreover you want to marry me only because she wants you to marry and settle in your life. I am sure that you never can forget about that Neeraja in your whole life." When they both were all alone in a room facing each others in two chairs, Thanuja expressed her feeling.

"You are right, I never can forget Neeraja in whole of my life." Anand said nodding his head. "It is also right the main reason for my intending to marry you is to make my Neeraja happy."

"Even after your expressing like this.........." Thanuja's face was filled with irritation. "..........how you are expecting that I do agree to live along with you?"

"There is something more I want to tell you." Aravind got off from the chair he sat and said. "My Neeraja's happiness is in my happiness. And my happiness is rooted in your happiness. Even Neeraja is always in some corner of my mind, I am confident that I can lead happy marital life with you. When it comes to marriage I just cannot think about any other girl except you just because Neeraja sees something alike in you and coming into you."

"She may never come into me again Aravind." Thanuja also got off from the chair she sat. "Once our marriage is over, her soul gets peace and she may dissolve into universe or take another birth."

"That's what I do exactly want. I want her soul to get peace and dissolve into universe or get another birth. I don't want her to remain as a soul and contact with me every now and then through you."

Thanuja remained silent as she did not know what to say.

"My mother struggled a lot to up-bring me and she is worrying so much as I remained like this worrying about that Neeraja. That Neeraja also is worrying a lot about me feeling fear that I may remain like this forever. If you marry me, you can make them both absolutely happy. Please think about it." there was sudden pleading expression in his face.

"If I marry you.........." looking straight into the face of Aravind, Thanuja asked him. "..........can you make me happy and treat me as your wife even you cannot forget about that Neeraja forever?"

"I am absolutely confident that I can make you happy to the maximum and treat you as my wife always."

"How......how you can prove that to me?" Thanuja knitted her brows together and she was still looking into the face of Aravind.

In an unexpected way Aravind took her into his both hands and kissed first straight on her lips and then both on her cheeks. "In this way. If you want, we can go some more further."

"Not necessary." The hug of Aravind was so much thrilling to her and Thanuja indeed has to put an effort to relieve herself from his hug. "You convinced me enough! I have no objection to our marriage."

Then without looking back she almost ran away from that place.

IT HAS BEEN DECIDED to perform the three marriages on the same day at the same venue and no one has objected to that. There was only one week time gap for the marriages from that day and in the morning of that Sunday all of them were assembled in the hall. Invitations have been sent to most of the relatives, friends and acquaintances and they were just verifying whether they missed anyone to invite.

"I have a close friend by name Malavika. Saritha knows about her very well and I think I mentioned about her at Anand also." Suddenly Malathi said.

"Yes, I know her very well." Saritha said. "She used to be quite supporting in your college days. He helped you and me also in many respects. The quite odd thing in her is; despite being post graduate in English, she has lot of interest in paranormal."

"You are right." Malathi nodded her head with a smile. "Even after settling in USA with her family, her interest in paranormal did not diminish even a little but increased even more. On some work, she visited India and is presently staying at her parents' house. She phoned to me yesterday and said to me that she is going to stay in India for one month or so. I invited her, her parents and brother also for the marriages. She said her parents and brother cannot but she sure does come. I asked her to come as soon as possible and she promised to come tomorrow itself when I expressed the problem of our house and wanted her help in that."

"You wanted her come early like that to give a solution to the spirits problem in our house?" Anand knitted his brows together.

"Absolutely yes." Malathi nodded her head. "She is a para psychologist and I am confident that she can hundred percent give a solution to our problem."

"In my opinion you did a very nice thing!" Sulochana said. "I wish she can give a solution to our problem."

"I hundred percent welcome her to our home. But we don't need her services as a para psychologist because there are never spirits or paranormal in my opinion." Saritha said.

"I just don't know how to understand you!" with an irritating expression Malathi looked into the face of Saritha. "You yourself have been possessed by that spirit on two occasions or so and behaved like that but cannot believe in spirits and paranormal?"

"I just cannot give any explanation at present for my odd behaviour and for the odd behaviour of our other family members but in my opinion......." Saritha tried to say something more.

"I just want to say the same thing that Sanjana said on that day." Malathi interrupted her and said. "If you cannot give a reasonable explanation for you people' odd behaviour, just keep your mouth shut and don't try to talk like this."

"But one thing here *vadina*." Prathap said. "Are you thinking that these spirits bear the presence of your friend in this home? She is an extra member and not matching with any member of Swaroop's family."

"If we think like that lifelong no person can come and stay in our house. Let her come and stay in our home. If these spirits don't let her stay, then itself we decide what to do." Sulochana said.

"Aunty is hundred percent right! As we are making alliances like this, it becomes quite normal a feature that the other people come and stay in our home. Anyhow that Malavika is a para psychologist and I think she can sure manage herself to stay here."

AS SHE PROMISED, MALAVIKA was in the home of Anand exactly by twelve in the morning the next day and warmly welcomed by Anand, Malathi, Saritha and Sulochana as the rest of the people were out on different works. In fact Anand and Prathap took long leave to look after the works of marriages. Prathap, Anand and Thanuja went out for purchase of several things for the three marriages.

By the time of lunch, everyone was present and after lunch, Malathi, Saritha, Thanuja and Malavika spent long time in Saritha's room and in that time Malathi, Saritha and Thanuja explained everything so clearly to Malavika. Malavika just listened and absorbed the information without making any comment. While it was going so, Anand, Sudarshan and Sulochana took rest in their respective rooms.

"I felt a lot when your life has been turned out like that Saritha. But now I am so happy that you are going to be settled in your life in this way. Anyhow tell me how is that guy? Did you hundred percent satisfy with him or is compromised just like previous time?" after settling in the sofa comfortably and sipping the coffee given by Malathi to her, Malavika asked her looking into her face who sat beside her in the sofa. At that time, all the family members of Anand were present. Malathi and Thanuja sat on the either side of Malavika and the rest sat in the chairs opposite to her.

"I should say he is compromised with me." Laughing with a happy expression in her face, Saritha said. "Despite the point he is married and has a son, he is handsome and manager of a reputed private bank. He owns that flat and said to me he has other properties also."

"That is indeed very much nice!" Malavika nodded her head. "But you people are performing three marriages at a time. Are not you feeling difficulty to do like that?" then she looked into the face of Sulochana.

"In fact we thought it would be convenient to us if we perform three marriages at one time. When the other sides also agreed to it, we are going ahead! How we are going to do that depends on god's grace." Sulochana said.

"Those marriages would certainly be wonderful affairs! You just be relaxed." Malavika said.

"You first tell me one thing!" suddenly interfering Malathi said. "I already explained everything in detail over phone and here also. Are you feeling the presence of the spirits here? As a para-psychologist I think that you can know the presence of the spirits if they are here."

"I already perceived the presence of the spirits here Malathi." Malavika said. "The good thing is; they are not angry or violent. In fact I can sense some peace and happiness in them. But I sensed ...." Malavika paused for a second before saying again. ".......one spirit among them is quite angry. But the remaining spirits are not allowing it to express its anger or do anything bad."

"That spirit is Swaroop I have no doubt in that." Malathi said angrily. "I already told you what he tried to do to Saritha possessing the body of Anand."

"You told me and I remember." Malavika nodded her head. "And I remember the fear you expressed also. Yes, there is sure a possibility that Swaroop tries to have Saritha after her marriage also."

On hearing that, the faces of the people there were filled with fearful expressions.

"You must solve this problem and make this house free of spirits. Malathi said you can do that." Sulochana said.

"I don't leave this house without solving your problem, you just feel relaxed!" Malavika laughed and said. "I stay until the marriages are over, make your house free of those spirits and then go."

"But one thing I want to say." Thanuja's face was with full of fear. "They did not let anyone stay in this house peacefully except us and we already explained to you why they let us stay here peacefully. You are someone not matching with any of that Swaroop's family members and you proclaimed like this also. I am really feeling fear what they would do to you now."

"I never do any harm to the spirits. I just settle their matters in an amicable and peaceful way. I am with a good intention and spirits have the ability to know the intentions in people. I am sure that they don't do any harm to me." Malavika paused for a second. "Moreover three of the spirits are getting their wishes satisfied and they are happy. There will be no problem whatsoever from their side. If there will be any problem it is from Swaroop and I am sure the other spirits don't let him to do anything bad to me also."

"Why did not they stop him from entering into my body and attempting something like that on Saritha?" Anand asked.

"The other spirits might not be in the home at that time, I cannot give any explanation to that." Malavika said.

"I think Malathi has explained to you the problem my husband and I are facing in this house because of the spirits of that Swaroop's parents." Sulochana's face was deeply blushed while saying that. "I think Swaroop's parents are enjoying doing it like that. Are you thinking that they do go away from here forsaking the pleasure they have been having like this? But it is so much bad and we both are feeling very much awkward for it."

"Yes, Malathi explained about this also to me and it is something I need to put my mind." Malavika said. "But for the present you don't worry about anything and just concentrate on the marriage work. I just keep my promise. I do leave this flat only after making it hundred percent spirits free." There was firmness in the voice of Malavika.

"But I cannot remain without saying one thing here." Saritha suddenly said. "I just cannot give any explanation for our odd behaviour now but in my firm opinion there are no spirits or paranormal."

"I already told you Saritha........." Malathi angrily said. "..........if you cannot explain why did you behave like that, just stop talking like this."

"Not just now, you are expressing your opinion like this from the moment I entered into your house. But just because of your non-believing spirits and paranormal, they are not going to become non-existent. Even whether there are spirits or not, there is paranormal or not, once I promise you I solve the problem of your house before I leave this place, there is no necessity of any discussion on it."

"Malavika aunty is absolutely right!" Thanuja said.

After that, those people some more time talked in themselves.

Chapter-9

"I just don't know how to understand any of this!" there was abundant fear in the face of Chakravarthy. "It was my family and Muchikund's family created the rumours that Swaroop's family members were still in that flat as spirits and we have been hearing their quarrels in the night time. As all his family members died on the day of their leaving itself, all the apartment members were in a state of fear and it has not become difficult to us to make them believe the rumours. We created fear like that in the tenants who came into that flat and made them run away from here. But......."

"........it is really very much fearsome that the spirits of the family members of Swaroop are still in that flat and do possess the family members of that Anand's family. They went to the extent to fix their marriages like that. Looking into the faces of that Anand's family, it seems that they don't like the alliances fixed because of those spirits. I just cannot understand how and why still that Anand's family are living in that flat!" Muchikund interrupted Chakravarthy and said.

"They are not tenants to run away like that but they are the owners of that flat buying it by paying sixty lakhs rupees. Now I am feeling so happy that I did not buy that flat." Mangal Rao said. "But I am just sorry for you both. You both were successful in creating rumours, making the residents of this apartment believe them and driving away the tenants of that flat as per my request but I did not pay as much as I promised to you."

"We are satisfied with the payment you made to us. With the hope to buy that flat at a very cheaper price you asked us to create rumours like that. Our idea wonderfully worked out but it has been bought by someone else." Chakravarthy said.

"I am just feeling happy that I did not buy that flat." Mangal Rao said. "I cannot live in a flat with my family which is full of spirits."

"Yes, you are right." Muchikund nodded his head. "I am feeling fear even to look at the expressions of that Anand's family members. I can say that they are suffering a lot in that flat in the hands of those spirits."

"I am thinking that it is better that we sell our flats and go somewhere else. The thought that there are spirits in my neighbouring flat itself creating tremors to my spine." Chakravathi said.

"My family also is just thinking like that." Muchikund said.

"Don't take hasty decisions. If you sell your flats now you have to sell them at a very cheaper price just like that Anand's vendor. So far those spirits in Anand's house did not do any harm to you. If they don't do any harm to you, why do you people try to flee? If ever there is any danger caused by those spirits to you people then itself we think about it." Mangal Rao suggested.

Chakravarthi and Muchikund looked into each other's faces and nodded their heads.

"NOW IS THE TIME THAT you keep the promise you made to me." When they both were together in the room of Malathi, she said to Malavika.

The three marriages were performed in the best way possible and all the family members were happy. First nights of the couples were also over and the gents themselves proved to their respective wives that their previous love affairs did not hamper even a little bit their sexual performance and their wives also made them so happy being active partners in sex to them. Sanjana also provided herself in the best way possible to Prathap and Prathap surprised when she became an equal active partner to him in sex.

One other thing that came into light and made them all absolutely happy was; Malathi became pregnant. Anand visited the doctor along with her, took precautions, prescription from the doctor and medicines from the medical shop before coming to home. As the marriages were also over, it has been ordered by all the family members to Malathi that she has to take absolute rest along with good food.

"On the night of this day itself I am going to do that." With a fixed expression in her face and determination in her voice Malavika said. "But only you, your family members and I are going to be present at that time, no one else. You have to manage it like that."

"I manage it like that." Malathi nodded her head and she managed it so in the night of that day.

"Now you five are going to sit in that sofa and I sit opposite to you. I invite those five spirits into your five bodies and once they come into your body I make them agree to leave this house forever." Malavika said.

"How you can say it for sure like that?" Malathi who sat in the chair beside Malavika said with anxiousness. "I don't think they do come into the bodies of these people at your request or command."

"You don't become anxious but watch what is going to happen." Looking into her face Malavika said. "And don't try to disturb whatever I am going to do."

"Alright then. I am not going to talk even a word more until all this is over." Malathi said and remained silent.

Malavika became straight in the chair she sat, closed her eyes for few seconds, then opened them and observed Sudarshan, Sulochana, Saritha, Thanuja and Prathap keenly for some more seconds before saying looking at the top of the house. "Oh, spirits in this house! I can know about your presence. I am your well wisher and I am here to do good to you. I invite you all to come into the respective body which you possessed before. I pray you all to come like that."

After her saying like that there are sudden change of expressions in the faces of the five sat in the sofa and Malathi was watching everything with surprise.

"I know that now you are in the people sitting opposite to me. All your wishes have been fulfilled. Now is the time to your spirits either to take another birth or dissolve in the universe. If you tell me what exactly you want whether to take birth again or mix yourself in the universe, I make arrangements for the same. I have the capability to do so." Malavika said just looking into the faces of the five one after one.

"I don't want to take another birth. My Saketh is happy with this girl. I want to be dissolved into universe." Saritha said

"I am also wishing just like that. My Aravind is happy with Thanuja and I am confident that they both can be happy like that forever. I also want to be dissolved in the universe." Thanuja said.

"I am also very much happy that my Sanjana got a very suitable guy to live along with. But ...." he paused for a second. "............I want to born as a baby to her. Can you manage it?"

Malavika sighed heavily and looked into the faces of Sulochana and Sudarshan. "What about you both?"

"It is very much good to me to have sex through this woman by possessing this man but......" Sudarshan paused for a second. "............I don't want to bother these couple anymore. I also want to be dissolved into universe."

"Only to prevent him to go to that watch man's wife or some other woman I have been providing that to him and I have no desire in sex. As my children and my daughter in law's sister also happy being settled in their lives, I don't see any reason to remain as a spirit anymore. The soon I get dissolve into universe, the better it is to me. I never like to have another birth."

"What about you? Are you also ready to put a stop to continue as a spirit by choosing either of the ways I suggested?" looking into the face of Anand, Malavika asked him.

"Until I fulfil my desire to have this woman........" looking into the face of Saritha with an expression of full desire Anand said. "........there is no question of my taking another birth or getting dissolved into universe. I must enjoy her beauty in the way I want."

On hearing that Malathi looked into the face of Malavika with sudden anxiousness.

"She is not your wife's sister whom you so much desired to have. She is someone else."

"But she is just like my wife's sister Sirisha and Sirisha preferred to possess her body seeing the similarity in her. Moreover Sirisha is dead and not available to me now to enjoy. I do have as much pleasure with this girl as I do have with Sirisha. On one occasion this girl could escape but not on the next occasion. At the first available opportunity I enjoy her in the way I want. I am sure that she would not agree with it and so it would be a brutal rape." Suddenly the expression in his face was sadistic and there was a crooked smile on his lips.

Malathi shuddered and her anxiousness became even more but Malavika was looking straight into the face of Anand without bothering about Malathi.

"If you do something like that Mr.Anand..........." suddenly there was firmness in the voice of Malavika. "............you do get life imprisonment or hanging punishment. Just remember that."

"That is going to happen to this guy but not to me." Anand laughed loudly. "No court can punish a spirit however much big mistake it may do."

"I am cautioning you Mr.Anand but not any spirit." With the same firmness in her voice, Malavika said. "It is just because there is no spirit in you now or at any time and it was you Mr.Anand who tried such ghastly thing on Saritha and it is only you who may try to commit such a thing on Saritha making the world believe it is not you but Swaroop's spirt in your body. But don't forget my warning! There is very much rigorous punishment for rape attempt or rape on women."

The whole environment there has become absolutely silent for few seconds and all the faces of the people there were filled with shocking expressions.

"No, it is not Anand.......it is Swaroop talking......" after few seconds Anand said with the same shocking expression in his face.

"If you don't agree yourself, it will not take much time to me to prove that there is no spirit in your body and it is only you, Mr.Anand, with whom I am talking." Malavika angrily said. "Not just you, none among you five have ever possessed by any spirit. You pretended and acted all the time as if you were possessed by spirits."

"How..........how the hell you can talk like that?" Malathi yelled loudly, got off from the chair and went before to Malavika. "How can you make a statement like that?"

Malavika also got off from the chair she sat and said looking straight into the face of Malathi. "I am para-psychologist Malathi. I can know the presence of spirits just in seconds if they are anywhere. The moment I have entered into your flat, what became so much clear to me was; there are no spirits in your flat. After hearing clearly what you and your sister along with that Thanuja said to me, what would have been possibly taking place struck me. There were specific reasons for these people pretending that they are being possessed by Swaroop's family members' spirits."

"Tell me what reasons you can assign that we acted as if possessed by spirits?" Prathap got off from the sofa and yelled angrily.

"Oh, I think it is Prathap now but not that Swaroop's brother!" Malavika laughed and said. "Yes, I give the reasons but I start with Saritha." Then Malathi looked into the face of Saritha. "By the time you people entered into the flat, there was a rumour that the spirits of Swaroop's family members were still in this flat. None of you do much belief in spirits and did not feel much fear to live in the house. After reading the diary written by Swaroop's wife, you people came to know lot many things. It was first Saritha who wanted to take advantage of that knowledge. Saketh, who loved by Swaroop's sister was not only handsome but has a good job and wealthy also. She just did not know when someone come forward to marry her and she thought it would be quite good if she could manage to marry Saketh. While she was thinking furiously how to do that, she got an idea from the fiction book she was reading at that time. Whatever confusion I have disappeared completely after I also read that book. In that book a girl's lover was dead and she has been forced to marry someone else. But that spirit of her lover used to possess her husband and behave like her love and did many things. Saritha thought how it would be if she goes to Saketh pretending as if she has been possessed by the spirit of his lover Sirisha. She did so and quite successful in that. It is not the wish of that Sirisha but the wish of Thanuja has been fulfilled, I must say."

"No. It is absolutely wrong. I never acted like that." Saritha also got off from the sofa and yelled loudly.

"You are psychologist Saritha not a para psychologist like me. It is you who expressed at me that there are no spirits and there is no paranormal. Then what I have said is not the possible explanation for your pretending as Swaroop's sister possessed you so? Anyhow there was not much wrong on your part. You make yourself settled and that Saketh also. It would be quite difficult to that Saketh without wife to him and mother to his son and you are the best girl to it. If we presume that Sirisha's spirit is somewhere now, she also feels so happy for it."

Saritha instantly slumped in the sofa, covered her face with both of her hands and burst into weeping.

"Prathap and Thanuja both got the inspiration from Saritha I think. Prathap joined in the same college where Rakesh studied and he might have made inquiries in the beginning about Rakesh's lover just with interest. Then he came to know that she was not only very much beautiful but all her properties have become free of litigations and she is very rich now. He did not know whether Saritha was indeed possessed by Swaroop's sister or acting like that but he decided to act as if possessed by Rakesh, Sanjana's lover and his ploy worked wonderfully. Tell me Prathap, am I wrong? If you still want to say I am wrong, there are ways that I can prove I am not wrong."

Prathap did not say anything but slumped in the sofa again, leaned back and closed his eyes.

"I think you can easily understand why Thanuja acted as if that Aravind's lover possessed her after hearing the explanation just I made. She just put an action all the time as if she did not interest in marrying that Aravind but from the very beginning she was interested in him. There is no surprise at all! Aravind is not only a handsome guy but a chartered accountant doing job in a big company without having any obligations except his mother. There is no doubt to her that her life would be wonderful if she becomes the wife of Aravind. Do you want to deny this Thanuja, just tell me?"

Thanuja did not say anything, picked her lower lip between her teeth frames, leaned back in the sofa and closed her eyes. Her face has become crimson red with anger and shame.

"Malathi told me about you also uncle. Once you came to know that Swaroop's father used to have it with that watch man's wife and after seeing Saritha's behaviour so, desire to have sex with young woman raised in you, an idea was formed in you and you successfully started implementing that. Aunty understood that you were going to that woman and having it with her and she did not know what to do. As Prathap, Thanuja, Saritha were already behaving as if they were possessed by spirits of Swaroop's family members, she found only one way to stop her husband from going to that woman. She started acting as if she was also possessed by the mother of Swaroop and forced uncle to have it with her."

"You are right! That was the only way I found to stop him from going to her. It was not so I have not got doubt on him and wanted to know the truth but I felt fear if I do so, the other three such behaviour also turned out to be acting! Whether it was acting or real, their lives were going to be settled in a beautiful way because of that. So I pretended as if I have been possessed by that Swaroop's mother and forced myself to believe that the others are really possessed by spirits." In a small voice Sulochana said.

"I think I made the point clear to you Malathi. All these people have some reason to pretend that each of the Swaroop's family members matched with her or his age possessed them but it is not so to you. You have no reason at all so you have not been possessed by that Swaroop's wife. If you think deep why you have not been possessed by Swaroop's wife just like others, you would have got the truth unearthed."

After her saying like that the whole environment was with absolute silence for sometime until Malathi came out of her shock and went near to Anand fast, holding his collar with both of her hands and shouted.

"How unethical and immoral you have become? Have you forgotten that a wife's sister is like a sister to you and Saritha is no different from Thanuja? Can you do something like that on Thanuja?"

"I am absolutely sorry." Hanging his head down Anand said. "I am feeling very much shame for what I did. Saritha is very much beautiful and I wanted to take advantage in the disguise that I have been possessed by that Swaroop. I promise you that I never do such mistake again. Pardon me for this time."

"My god........I just don't know what to do?" Malathi suddenly stood straight, hold her head with both of her hands and about to fell back but then not just Malavika, all the others came there and supported her.

"Whatever events have taken place, have taken place. The lives of Prathap, Thanuja and Saritha settled in a beautiful way and we are all happy. Every person on earth does mistakes and we have to give chance to them to correct themselves and move in a right way. Anand and his father both did mistakes but we give them chance to mend themselves. If they can't, future will decide what should happen to them."

Once they were all settled in the sofa and chairs in the hall again, Malavika said.

"I never do such type of a mistake again! I don't let such bad thoughts enter into my mind ever." With a regretful expression in his face Anand said which appeared genuine to all of them.

"I am also giving the same word. I never do go to another woman for sex. I have it with my wife only providing she agrees to it." there was such a genuine expression in the face of Sudarshan also.

Immediately there was silence and it was Malathi who was adjusted herself to the new developments and broke that silence by saying.

"Then what about the residents here hearing of the voices of Swaroop's family from this flat even after their death also? Why those who came into this flat as tenants after Swaroop's family's death, could not stay here even for one week?"

"I am thinking taking advantage of the weird death like that of Swaroop's family, some people created rumours so to buy this flat at very cheap price. As the residents here were already disturbed by the ghastly death of Swaroop's family like that, they readily believed the rumours created so. Whoever created those rumours systematically let the tenants knew about them and made them felt fear to their bones. As they were just tenants but not owners, they felt better to vacate this flat rather than staying in it. But quite unluckily whoever created those rumours to get this flat quite cheap lost that chance as you people have got it like this."

"That much is true I must say." Forgetting about the recent happenings Malathi laughed happily and said. "We have to consider ourselves lucky."

"I agree with that." Malavika nodded her head and said.

"Then everything is alright and we need not bother about anything." Sulochana said.

Once again there was silence and this time there were happy expressions in the faces of the people there.

"I kept my promise, did not I? I made your house absolutely spirits free before I leave this place, is it is not?" after few seconds breaking that silence Malavika asked Malathi looking into her face.

"Yes, you did." Malathi smiled and said.

As you are here, I hope that you read the novel. Thank you very much that you preferred to read my novel. If you bother to write a review also, I shall be so much grateful and thankful to you.

Charitha was desperate to save her family from its financial crisis and was worrying too much as she could not do that with the meagre income she was having through her small job. She just did not like her friend Prameela's helping her financially time and again but she could not deny as there was no other way at all except that to come over at least some of that predicament. When she could not get a good job anywhere with a better salary and when she could not find any other way to help her family, she got the chance to act in a movie with forty lakhs rupees remuneration. As it was a sexy movie and there would be lot of exposing also, it has indeed become a delicious predicament to Charitha to act in that move to save her family from that financial crisis. What was the experience of Charitha while she was acting in that movie as she not only has any experience in acting but no interest whatsoever in acting till that moment is the story of this book 'Delicious Predicament'.

Also by Kotra Siva Rama Krishna

Two Strangers On The Bed
A Girl's Conflict
Enna
Strawberry
Dusk
Just Relax!
Delicious Predicament
Nirupama
Half Opened Doors
Lovenest
Moonshine
Scarecrow
Closed Doors
Disturbed
Handfuls of Sand
Mansion of Illusions
Rain Flower
Rose Garden
Sand Dunes
Snow Flower
Split Personality
Being Possessed
Objection Sustained
House of Delusions
Rustle in the Leaves

Sasikala
Amaswitha
English Grammar Simplifier
Wisps of Smoke
Shadow in the Mirror
Love is Dangerous with a Stranger
Shadow of a Spirit
Unwanted Guests